T0247432

Our Best Love Story

Mario Levi

OUR BEST LOVE STORY

Translated from the Turkish by Zeynep Beler

DALKEY ARCHIVE PRESS

Originally published in Turkish by AFA Yayıncılık as *En Güzel Aşk Hikayemiz* in 1992.

Copyright © 1992 by Mario Levi
Translation copyright © 2018 by Zeynep Beler
First Dalkey Archive edition, 2018.

Library of Congress Cataloging-in-Publication Data
Names: Levi, Mario, 1957- author. | Beler, Zeynep, translator.
Title: Our best love story / Mario Levi ; translated by Zeynep Beler.
Other titles: En gèuzel aðsk hikãayemiz. English
Description: First Dalkey Archive edition. | Victoria, TX : Dalkey Archive Press, [2017] | Originally published in Turkish by AFA Yayincilik as En gèuzel aðsk hikãayemiz in 1992.Identifiers: LCCN 2017048196 | ISBN 9781628972306 (pbk. : alk. paper)
Classification: LCC PL248.L45 E513 2017 | DDC 894/.3534--dc23
LC record available at https://lccn.loc.gov/2017048196

www.dalkeyarchive.com
Victoria, TX / McLean, IL / Dublin

Dalkey Archive Press publications are, in part, made possible through the support of the University of Houston-Victoria and its programs in creative writing, publishing, and translation.

Printed on permanent/durable acid-free paper

CONTENTS

Foreword to the Fifth Edition   xi

1	A Meeting in the Shelter	3
2	The Tunnel	15
3	An Inferno with Suad	23
4	Waves, or the Pebbles of Max von Sydow	26
5	Hesitation	32
6	Your Photograph toward Me	33
7	Threshold	35
8	Your Journeys after So Much Downpour	37
9	Silence	42
10	The Arab's Coffeehouse, Shores, Train Whistles	43
11	The Earthquake Inside	47
12	The Chinese Restaurant	48
13	A Summer's Evening in Sintra	52
14	Your Face, Left to Me	55
15	The Old Geography of Solitude	58
16	Walking in a Mirror	59
17	A Song with Amalia	62
18	Melancholy, the Qanun, Afternoon, and Other Such Things	63
19	You Were Prisoners to Deception	65
20	Cognac Glasses on the Beach	66
21	Or, the Boundaries of the Manuscript	69
22	My Impromptu Insomnia	71
23	Eşref Bey Prepares for a Text	72
24	Images, Fear, and Imaginary Parenthetical Stories	77
25	Faces, the Streets, Hopeless Shadow Theaters	79
26	The Wind that Wraps around the Manuscript	82
27	Action, My Friend, Mere Action	83
28	Appearing As Though Living	86

29	An Old, Age-Old Old Dream	90
30	If You Only Knew	93
31	If That Resentment, That Call, That Isolation Had Never Been	96
32	A Hell Springs Then to My Mind	98
33	Separations, or What Hides in Hidayet's Painting	99
34	My Lie, My Captivity, a True "Bird on a Wire"	105
35	Of Drinks, Evenings, and Getting Lost on the Way Home	112
36	If You Only Knew Why Selami Disappeared	117
37	Do We Believe This Woman?	122
38	New Loves, New Disappointments	126
39	Epilogue, or After a Delayed Visit	128
40	Eternal Game, Eternal Death	150
41	Old Games, Old Narratives	156
42	That Spell, That Passion, That Deadly Journey	159

Foreword to the Fifth Edition

The period that this book was written in coincides with one of the most jarring emotional ruptures I've ever experienced. The story flowed out on its own, with barely any preliminary work, or, to be more accurate, presented and imposed its own narration in the process of being written. Ripples that would later engender other stories and relationships first came to life here. I remember very clearly that when I punctuated the last word I was overcome by a feeling of discontinuity and incompleteness. I had attempted to verbalize a love affair, but what I really felt was the melancholy, deficiency, and unavoidable tension most of us feel when we love . . . I also would never have imagined in those days that years later I'd undertake writing yet another love story. One has to experience it and experience it again to finally begin to comprehend. Now, when I look back on what I experienced, of what I was capable, I won't refrain from declaring that this long story or narration can be read as a kind of preliminary work for *Lunapark Kapandı*. That wasn't my intent in the beginning, of course. How could I have predicted what would be stirred up within me? The procession of years, however, necessitated such a rendezvous. In that sense it's possible to read this book as both an autonomous manuscript showcasing my observations during a certain period and as a critical draft in the chronicle of *Lunapark Kapandı* . . . those who carefully undertake a reading of this novel about a decade and a half after it was written, that I chance to present to the reader without improving a single line, will be able to locate it exactly and make the right connections, I'm sure of it. Despite having been dubbed "difficult" by many readers, the book went through four editions. Now, with this fifth edition I want to hope that it will reach new, different people. Hoping, hoping once again . . . the apprehensive longing to communicate, to make oneself heard . . . is that not reason enough to go on?

1
A Meeting in the Shelter

IN THIS NEW BOOK, **you once again confront us with the antici-**
pated and at times timeworn paths and voyages, Mario Levi.
That voice, or person, that desire—so to speak—seems to be
sought once again in this novella as an idiosyncratic experi-
ment in style. We may find the chance to explore the reasons
for such resistance in the numerous facets of the conversation
that could plausibly take shape between us. First, however,
I'd like to enter this extensive loneliness through another
door, a door of significance I have difficulty ignoring. Why
a love story, and one so reckless and bound to appear rather
neurotic to most at that, in a world where so much mundan-
ity and superficiality is approved, where nuance and, even
more regrettably, poetry fade and are deemed superfluous?

In the face of so much time, destruction or, in the briefest terms,
words, was it really a love story I attempted to tell in this book,
one that could appear meaningless or inconsistent to most? I
could take the easy way out by simply replying in the affirma-
tive, claiming: because no one writes the kind of love story that
I yearn and long for, and no one wants to. As you pointed out
in your question, in a world where superficiality is approved and
given free rein over all power structures, such passion could,
despite all its risks, present a sliver of hope in the spirit of snub-
bing losses, defeats, and mounting self-immolations. Regarding
the circumstances in which this adventure was born, then beginning somehow to fade and turn into estrangement and longing,
it would've been possible to point out that love is fundamentally

and intrinsically a journey from one displeasure to another and one dead end to another; and to speak of archaic investigations into the subject. Love, in all its possibilities, legends, and fantasies, could've appeared to be an ever-postponed departure. With that said, it isn't possible for me to evade or, to be more precise, ignore my hesitation in setting out to answer your question with only a few words. In this story, love was only an aspect of recklessness and human disconnection. At unexpected times I was often required to relive certain disappointments.

So you set out from a small escapade, a brief affair, and arrived at the lineaments of an ancient heartbreak.

Or: after a certain point you lose track of what time it is, at what point in a dream you stand, or what version of reality you're experiencing. Dreaming was a sort of vanishment, an inability to return, while reality was decidedly untrustworthy. There before you was a new possibility, and you tried to make the voice heard while preserving the mistake.

And yet there's never any need for those words in such an unexpected, unpracticed affair. A new day dawns and you try and find new covers and new masks for your rejection.

True. Yet aren't many texts that relate heartbreak commenced to overcome such defeats, even if only for a little while?

How, then, did you conceive of your defeats at this point? In other words, as you set out on this long text, what disappointments or, as you often put it, dilemmas, did you start from?

That's an unsettling question, because after a certain point it pushes one to explain, expose, and gradually interpret a long-completed text. It makes you question yourself once more as to what point of the adventure you stand at. You try to explain that you're more disposed to multiple readings and not just one, you say: the games are over, I have no more claims to interpretation. For you dream that what you wrote was never-ending, that others picked up where you left off. That must be the reason I find ambiguity so bewitching. I wish you knew how beautiful it is to dream that a book can move from one person to another.

It *is* a dream, yes, but in my opinion what is in question here is *only* a dream. What's more, it carries massive, absolutely colossal risks. Did you ever stop to consider, for instance, that such a reading might bring the book somewhere completely different from where you imagined in the beginning, or think you've brought it now, that it might take it altogether out of your reach?

How could I not consider that? To be honest, I'd braced myself for this a long time ago. When longing for a connection or answering a call despite all hesitancy, you must be open to all kinds of joy or remorse. At this stage, however, it's also possible to approach things from another angle. You imagine, for instance, that you can confront a complete stranger within a text, within a sum of sentences. She sees you but you can't see her. You talk of a life, a heartbreak, and she's simply and totally silent, or she does speak, or makes as if to speak, to attempt to reply to your call in the way you expect her to. Yet even if there is a reply, even if the echo of that voice tries to reach you, you hear nothing. In the end this silence, this polyphonic silence, takes you back to that dream world that you love so dearly. There you are alone with a familiar theme, bringing to your mind the poems, street musicians, incense fumes, whores of the harbor, the hookah parties you never experienced as wantonly as you would've liked and the letters you never wrote as often as you would've wished. It's the joy of an unexpected journey; the kind of joy that gives you the freedom to take only what you want in the name of a brand-new sentence.

A brand-new kind of joy, yes. To think of that now and then, to recall it some way or another, even that provides some measure of relief. Yet if you ask me, you push the scenario a little too far. In other words, no one person is that concerned with another.

You may be right. But think about it, what else is left to us but to seek out a long poem or transform recklessness into hope, no matter how small, or into the ragtag sum of a few joys? There comes a moment, ultimately, in which the pain of defeat makes itself felt to us in more concrete terms than ever. All that's left is the consolation that we had risked or are capable of risking a struggle or a battle even if only in the sense of rowing upstream. For as long as you're in transit, you are under obligation to trust something you may always have difficulty naming or describing, somehow, despite everything.

Yet some of your experiences on this passage tell us that you undertake great defeats on purpose and steadily make them your own. What you encounter as you trace the way to some small joy seems to estrange you further from her or that lost paradise, so to speak. Who knows, perhaps the walk has turned into a backward walk, a kind of stepping backward, or a progress toward your own self, and *only* yourself. The Narrator takes a chance and, unaccepting of his suggested place in the text, chooses to seek sanctuary with an unknown lover. Discovering too late, at any rate, the dilemma that lies therein, that is to say, the impossibility of finding sanctuary in a lover, he also fails for some reason to sense the distastefulness of wishing to, of sincerely voicing the wish, fails to feel the haughtiness in imposing himself on another. Yet when you think about it, it's all so obvious.

If what you say is true, it must be considered that advancing toward another with all this in mind is soothing, if not altogether reassuring. Yet I've always been of the mind that despite everything, despite all experienced or potential emotion, one can never be completely prepared for another person in a relationship, let alone a love adventure. A single smile, a whiff of scent, or a few words can transform that so-called sedentariness, shake it to the core. The narrator knew that the only way this affair could end was in heartbreak, if you ask me. Here as always, as everywhere else, we had needs, willful self-deceptions, and most importantly, inevitabilities.

Isn't that rather fatalistic?

You're free to interpret it as you wish. I don't think such approaches are capable of affecting the underlying meaning of the manuscript. At this point in time, however, in the name of maintaining tension, I feel we would do well to remember that words are untrustworthy and liable to lead us to very different associations.

It seems as though you expend an inordinate amount of effort seeking sanctuary in a manuscript that is, at times, allied with your loneliness, and, at other times, with your desire to find a lover. After a time you resume your pursuit with seemingly unending sentences, appearing to entice readers to get lost in them with no way of returning. How do you feel you have the right, or what experience do you imagine grants you the right?

Your appraisals necessitate a long explanation, indeed, increasingly, an interpretation. I worry, for instance, that in this tale of refuge, a hasty approach may prove to be downright hazardous. The longing in question is old, a very old longing, in fact. At this level I must stress once more that there are truths I prefer not to hide behind a curtain of obscurity, meetings and partings I prefer to see left open to possibility, and certain relationships,

places, or people I wouldn't enjoy seeing end up as a sum of
sentences. The fact that certain people are called upon to be lost
inside sentences might well be explained by the effort to prolong
this yearning despite all. When that happens, I'm assailed by the
feeling that I'm a stranger to the story and that I can only write
it with the help of the one whose existence and attentiveness I
more or less am sure of and that, in other words, I'll never be
able to finish it—deliberately repeating myself, I wish to point
out that in this way, the writing adventure can be enriched in a
totally new dimension. Despite this minuscule yet deeply meaningful bliss, I now also feel the discomfort of having agreed to
this interview. It means facing another new and entirely unnecessary problem. A new problem, or an unavoidable obligation
to explain. All else aside, we have many reasons to assume that
what is being said here is in no way geared toward explaining
the book. At most, a scrutiny or, if you will, an interrogation
is being carried out in an unorthodox manner. The real danger stems from the fact that I undertake this trifling adventure
with you. Your surprise at my consenting to this interview then
becomes more understandable. We understand each other well,
regrettably. Up until this day, we've been known to take great
risks together in the name of searching for our identity. Just try
and recall the texts in which we've met before, the guises we've
met under, the emotions.

**Searching for identity, trying to externalize it out of the blue:
it does seem that we try to approach one another through
words. Perhaps we're only trying to chase that hope once
more. Yet as you see, we're once again at the same junc-
ture, sharing the same obligation or the same sedentariness.
Ultimately, is that not a kind of small death? Are these dead
ends and isolations not valid for everyone who lives in the
orbit of certain words, who is prisoner to certain vicious
cycles?**

They could be. That could be why I feel that "another" might have been able to go in a completely different direction with this interview. When we hold back from asking questions, when we allow the magic of words to sweep us off our feet and when, most of all, we hold off answering these questions for as long as we can, it all gains a new and completely different meaning.

Questions and the lack of answers. Is it once more the departure from a question, followed by the arrival at another, that you speak of? For instance, what is the difference between this story's initial destination and ultimate terminus? Had you hoped to give new meaning to an adventure by heading from deadlock to deadlock, to unexpected, unconsidered impasses?

Of course. After all, I've never lost that matchless sense of adventure within, despite the lack of meaning, the impasse. Yet despite everything, despite all the times I steeled myself to return to those small hopes, I never envisioned for this story a certain place, an ending or, to be perfectly honest, a resolution. In those formative first days there was no knowing how things would progress, there couldn't have been, you understand. The only thing certain, as always, was the journey to a possibility, the gradual forming of a sentence. We could only trust our instincts, in any case we had no choice. Besides, it isn't even all over yet. If you ask me, it's still a long, long way off from being complete. There are many more lives to live before the end.

I suppose, in that case, that in spite of our wishes, our interview in this book will be left incomplete just like all our other encounters, hopefully to be continued in a different time or emotional landscape.

Incomplete and lacking. In spite of all the people who carry us into the future, all obligatory postponements. Incomplete and lacking, yes. Yet I ask you, what beloved story has ever been completed in the actual sense? Have we not often crossed over with the protagonists of certain stories into brand-new inner adventures?

It seems to me that you somewhat intentionally sustain a never-ending unease, an obsession with defeat or, most significantly, a certain bitterness. Everything aside, despite all the words and searching, you seem to be stubbornly hiding something that I'm finding hard to define.

It's true that I hide something, keep something to myself, though not always in full awareness. I honestly don't know what it is I hide, or how to explain it. That secretiveness, that obscurity, is in my opinion still preferable to all instant solutions, the superficialities that bind together great crowds of people and prop up so-called unshakable truths. There's no need for regret, however. Neither this adventure nor the unease we attempt to define would or could have any meaning otherwise. To the judgment that I'm obsessed with defeat, on the other hand, I believe only a long and detailed response would do justice. It feels like a provocation, a trap. I find the concept of defeat too valuable to allow it to be subjected to an artless and superficial discussion. I'll settle for merely pointing out that you stubbornly resist understanding and, more importantly, questioning certain truths because you fear confronting yourself. Furthermore, I'm not entirely comfortable with the notion that I'm bitter. If that were the case, I'd have withdrawn into my own corner, no, into my silence like those protagonists of old-time tales with their surprise appearances in one's own long story . No, I'm not bitter. If you had instead accused me of being hurt, however, now that would have been an appraisal I couldn't easily have talked my way out of. I'm either hurt or crushed by the knowledge that I'll never communicate to another all my words, longings, or my self in the way I desire; never share the sadness of my experiences or my failure to make the most of life, with all the directness or spontaneity of the events that brought me here; won't even be able to recognize or inhabit myself one day soon in one of the unexpected yet predestined stops in this journey. No notion, as you see, is as easy to live down as one may expect; no truth or judgment as reliable. If you wish, we may at this point return to the mystery that you were having trouble defining. Briefly recall that moment that we each know well and must experience at least a few times in our lifetimes, in which we're overtaken by a sort of stillness, the need to go far, far away. On one side is abandonment, on the other enterprise. Where is the who, where are *you*, by what path and whom do you long to reach? Do you find yourself in a contradiction or a compulsion to self-defend? Is it a divergence of roads, such as in said manuscript, that you're confronted with, or your imprisonment by loneliness?

You seem inclined to constantly remind us that we live inside a vicious cycle. In that case, many tales must be considered alongside the power of lies and illusion.

Honestly, it was an illusion and a funny little lie that brought us to the present, no matter our actions. No reality was our reality in the actual sense, because no reality ever confronted us in its naked glory, leaving no room for doubt. The secrecy you've just tried to touch upon always existed, a deception that constantly defined our characters. Who but you yourself can know what sentence, word, punctuation mark, or dreamlike parenthetical annotation you kept alive in your consciousness after you had read the book, at times with a small joy and at others with a sadness I assume you're accustomed to? Would you be able to describe to your heart's desire, despite the price you've paid, your progress toward one you met unexpectedly or might meet—the colors, the smells, the possibilities?

I don't know, I just don't know. Yet here we are, whatever this is; we're here. We're at the same place, inside the same manuscript. Just like everyone who is listening to us now,

observing us silently. Inside the same manuscript, with our masks and our vulnerability we try so hard to ignore and cannot admit.

You do know it was complicit.

Partners in crime, yes. A complicity: perhaps that word signals the removal of all masks in the end.

The masks will never fall, rest assured. As long as these words and memories and regressions exist, they'll never fall.

If only we could define where we stand. If we could only explain that we yearn to achieve and experience entirely different things.

If we could only know where we stand . . . careful, such words may be used against you at a time you least expect.

It appears to me that you yourself don't know the answer to the question embedded here. You evade. Really, you're incapable of anything other than evading, running. Is that why you wished to leave everything behind, even after all the upheavals?

Words, words, only words. We never knew where we stood, or perhaps never managed to explain. Yet it seems that we should have gone through all of this anyhow. In other words, what we struggled to share was only an inescapable journey. We were at a stop in a long, tremendously long journey that we could have gone on without knowing about it. To live out the book, the story we had pined for for years, was postponed to an ambiguous date as usual.

To be caught up in a question, to dare move along the breadth of a question despite all the risks. As you see, I've never easily evaded the assault of the words, the possibilities, or the dreams that have so often governed my life. It would be superfluous to even comment that this interview won't end here or in this way, that it is to be resumed in a different incarnation of this bizarre story. Relaying after the fact the following events that you'll soon read, or to be more accurate, witness; to order them after some fashion, was no little predicament, truth be told. Now, the result I'm faced with after all this effort and hope, I must admit, is more than a little distressing. Various more recent occurrences and the ones left untold to avoid endangering, or at least encumbering, certain lives, spark in me the desire to start it all from scratch. And yet after a period of pondering and turning inward, to whatever extent I can manage, futility ultimately greets me in all its harshness. A different ordering of events might as well have opened up a different story and, after a certain point, this search might have cracked open the door to a different sort of encounter or a rendezvous, and we could have tried anew to be different people entirely. When I consider the hellishness of the gaze I'm sure you know so well, however, or the fact that we will always be strangers to every new longing or, even more importantly, that you'll never be able to describe to a friend, a prospective friend who was born blind, the color red, *your* red, that you love so much, I feel like this is a battle not worth revisiting. Perhaps the adventure of writing has the same taste as describing that red, that infinite red, to such a friend, is what I tell myself in such situations. It then embarrassingly occurs to me that the red has never been successfully relayed to me either, from another perspective, or in the light of another longing. Once more I yearn to embrace a certain night, a phone call, a song, or simply a sentence. Indeed, I can never give up on the dream of taking refuge in a sentence. A way out must exist after all this time, I say to myself, where evocations or inner storms or convulsions cannot ever be told or shared with another. I long to set out on a journey by myself once again: a journey toward a new manuscript or an utterly different story. It appears that, in this case, only one question remains. You remember the fear, that deeply familiar quandary. Was it possible to convey it, you ask yourself, was it possible to convey to your own self your insecurity inside this treacherous shelter? In that moment a street appears to flicker into view, bringing to your mind afresh the rain, the coast, the smell of fall. A wry smile spreads across your lips. You let everything go.

2
The Tunnel

I CAN'T REMEMBER NOW when I first thought of the irresistible pull of suicide, the unreliability of set rules of ethics, the hypocrisies that tradition was expected to deal with, the absolute necessity to kill a man before one dies, the night journeys, the train stations, the endless loneliness of highway motels, the favorite character of an earlier novel accompanying a new one, the journey of my novel or to never finish a sentence, to keep constantly changing a text within the flow of time, to track down some small joy, though with decided hesitation, despite a hopefulness that's hard to define. Really I know that by mentioning the many long years that have passed, I'll affect many prospective friends in a myriad of ways. After all, such words allow one to move toward a small crack in the door with just a little hope, to once more navigate those evocations, those silent, suppressed storms. After such a sentence, one may easily speak of defeat, disenchantment, lost paradises, and awful passions; and even if no enthusiasms or disappointments come to the fore, numerous people or regrets may be encountered. At this stage, however, I'm reminded of a detail miles beyond these possibilities, just a detail. A truth that I touch upon often in conversation with people I assume I can trust or in my ridiculous repeating of myself; a truth that, so to speak, I'm still fooled by though I would really rather not be: there are hurts that can only be relayed long, long after they have been overcome, that is, after the deepest darkness has been experienced. During these days that I'm content to merely ask the questions, that I accept my own self-loathing more with each passing day, that I can no longer insist on interrogation as much as I used to, I now think the exact opposite of what I once wished to convey: that, despite what is widely assumed, some hurts can never be overcome, will never be overcome, that what is related is merely the translation of those hurts into a different form in our imaginations. In such situations, memories and real people, words and the inability to communicate, just like in many other tales I think I more or less experienced, thoroughly bleed together. If I could only distance myself now and then from these strange relationships, expectations, the pain of unmade phone calls or fruitless, quotidian designs, if I could leave behind what I've done so far and try to live out an old, very old tale in my own way, for instance camping out in a hotel that reeks partly of alcohol and partly of bathhouse, in an unknown town that I abruptly set out to after picking it out on the map and the next day, accompanied by the residue of poetry inside me, having breakfast at the coffeehouse in the town square, returning to where I will be returning, my streets leading to the seaside, my fish shop that sells the freshest octopuses, my movie escapades and, in short, to this city that I love less with each passing day with brand-new and special images, and to externalize it all somehow, to knowingly prolong the adventures of those old offences without broadcasting my fight to make certain kinds of loneliness more tolerable—I think to myself then. At the same time, this yearning also necessitates remembering once more and reliving, with a measure of regret, derangement, and embarrassment, the things I've been through in this strange place these past few years, when in fact, to be perfectly honest, I feel like recounting neither the evening when the batty Janin, lonely and weathering her own little storm, suddenly stood at her window, applauding those who had cast her out, nor Celine's song that has always stayed with me, nor my parting of ways with Çalık even despite our voyage of emotions, nor the great difficulties I once endured to cook leek dumplings, nor the letters I was never able to write. I don't wish to recall once more the days of my mandatory military service, the addresses of so many whorehouses, my weakness for large-breasted women, and my loathing for condoms. These are old stories, each vastly wounding in and of itself. On the other hand, I'm of the opinion that childish fancies such as abruptly taking wing and flying off to eternity or discovering an inconceivable life on an ignored star or vanishing, even if briefly, into any dream I desire, becoming without warning an invisible man or experiencing a kind of love somewhere, anywhere on this earth, the kind that will never end or fade, wouldn't go far by way of convincing anyone. To tell the truth, I myself have no consistent excuse for dreaming of a love that gives one hope for an endless, genuine, and unknowable future, or of never returning from a person in hopes of being granted eternity. Yet in a world where the number of those who can't find the time to perceive tiny truths, beautiful in their simplicity, due to their many pressing (!) problems, increases with each passing day, possessing the heart of a child is alluring and desirable no matter what, in my opinion. It's the oldest of games, to be sure: a game or a fancy that remains unfinished despite all the relationships and more importantly, footsoreness. Fancies, yes: fancies that carry us from person to person and from seemingly forgotten story to completely dissimilar story and at other times to a question, an unexpectedly simple question. To tell the truth, I'm not as afraid as I used to be of living with and stubbornly maintaining these dreams. The day comes when one can sense whom one will run into somewhere along the way, learning to live with danger whether one likes it or not. Yet I still don't mean to speak of frustration, disappointment, or fruitless self-restraint. I don't know where this long manuscript will take me, but at this time I imagine starting everything over again in sheer

vulnerability, I long to chase diverse details and small joys
once again. I don't wish now to dwell on how this city that
I've lived in for years, that I'm practically obliged to live in
and to keep returning to, can recite the poetry of a sea, a
coast, a mackerel, and, more significantly, a handful of rum
taverns utterly different from the ones here today, how people were dragged from their homes one unexpected evening
and severed from their daily lives and customs because of
their ideas or their roots, to be exiled without hope of return,
the days when books were hidden away as elements of crime,
the ones who, in the name of their political views, picked
one injustice in favor of another, submitted to one fanaticism
in favor of another and all the rest of this interminable sleep
paralysis. I often prefer, due to a kind of love that's rather
hard to explain, to keep to myself that this city's history
contains many instances of such disgrace. In such times the
city seems to leave my insides, to desert me, and I'm plagued
with apprehension that my returns unavoidably tend toward
estrangement or an inner exile that I'm afraid I can't relate
easily. I know very well by now that I can't restrain my
attachment to this journey, this return to the self, this sea,
these streets or the histories of their odors. It's doubtless a
story that has been experienced before, tried, was missed; a
story that's tantamount to an adventure of dead ends and
dejectedness. Yet no matter the hopes provoked by a sentence
or the contents of a parenthesis or the ambiguity of a text,
especially its openness to questioning, one must ultimately
experience one's own story, journey, and increasing solitude.
All the same, the problem now comes down to much more
than my incessant navel-gazing, my deliberation on the
clues, extrapolations, or possibilities of a life. For I was
unceremoniously, unexpectedly abandoned by the narrator
who had accompanied me on this ill-advised journey over
the years with silent solidarity, at a point in a story that I
was not at all prepared for; left alone with my words, my

nakedness, and all my failures. I know that my angle of
approach to the events I'm going through today may be
regarded by many as strange, even erroneous. Many may be
impelled to explain my attitude, at the same time confirming
the apprehensions of my grandmother, as the predictable
and natural results of my overzealous reading. Yet no matter
what the approach, I'm of the feeling that I've been betrayed
at this point in the story in a manner that was wholly
uncalled for. This partnership had, for better or for worse,
been forging ahead, or had seemed to be, in spite of all odds.
The conditions had been established and it looked as if the
games would always be played in this manner and, though
I can't say why, my Narrator appeared to have accepted with
all maturity this role that had been suggested to him. I'd be
lying if I said such ease wasn't suspect, or that from time to
time questions wouldn't begin to nag at me. Was I face-to-
face, for instance, with a clandestine plan of action devised
by the Narrator? Was each agreement or each silent smile the
sign of a secret uprising? Would there, at some point, be
some sort of exchange of power? Had we always lied to one
another, as is the case with every bloodless relationship?
Were we simply a lie, in other words, that extended from
those days to the present? As you can see, the questions
turned inward in this partnership as they always did, or
inclined to. Yet from the viewpoint of outsiders we were har-
monious in a surprising or, even more alarmingly, covetable
way. The niche afforded to us seemed to gain meaning and
deserve attention for this very reason. In the end, this state
of affairs engendered a great deception and an inescapable
delusion. There were many who thought the experiences of
my Narrator in the stories to be my own memories and
chronicles. There were others who went as far as to suggest
an identity crisis or a conflicted character. In truth, it wasn't
as if we hadn't anticipated the risk in the early days. I suppose that was also partly the reason that we chose to hide

our partnership over the years, incessantly postponing appearing together before friends whose presence we couldn't do without. Those were the days during which, despite the queries and the irrepressible suspicions, our unshakeable solidarity began. We were the only ones who were aware, and would ever be aware, of the margin of pretense in a story, one that increasingly demanded to be written with each passing day, if you get my drift. In those days, the past and the present were united, possibilities, yearnings, defeats, and rebirths all bled into one another. The dangerous investigations into the past also, in a way, functioned as forays into days that were presently being lived, or somehow would be. A silent, seemingly unshakeable kind of solidarity. It was just another form of escape, naturally. For one to live out a story to the last sediment of one's strength, however, for one to hold onto a world one would do anything to grasp and breathe in, one must search for oneself in the face of all of one's desperation; one must at times dare to go into full battle, never letting go of one's dreams. All the same, in the dark enclave of relationships, unexpected developments are bound to catch one totally off guard, if not completely defenseless. In those days I couldn't have found a better way to explain the absconding of my Narrator from my supervision after so many years, to abruptly embark on a brand-new voyage, and the state that it put me in. Naturally, in companionship or obligatory cohabitation, we had to be open to many possibilities, but back then there was a major problem that could not be ignored and awaited solution no matter what it took. For we were up against a passion that didn't work, the fact of which had been evident from the start; we must accept and swallow this defeat, this forced reversal that was fast turning into a dead end. The worst part was that these developments had been entirely out of my hands, as I just tried to point out; they had happened in spite of me. A character of mine, whose friendship I was ecstatic about having finally earned, had notified me one morning while I was conducting some small research on the uses of the semicolon. It was too late—my Narrator, who had taken advantage of my extended hiatus from story writing, had absconded, I daresay without hope of return, to an unknown manuscript, abandoning every proposal for a sentence, every search for a word, or exercise in solitude. It was an unexpected rejection. I had been equal with almost all of my characters in status, as a spectator who couldn't intervene in the game no matter how much he would have liked. Selami and I had spoken at length about how the only possible outcome for this affair was heartbreak. Yet, as I mentioned before, the rules of the game had been designed in a much different way in those days than you would have thought or could ever imagine. In that game, as in all games that we were left out of or banished from, silence was obligatory. All the events that you're about to be confronted with, though only through clues—only clues and their interpretations—were all played by these rules. What was said was said, and what was unsaid remained an offense, a reprieve, or a possibility.

The expected return took place after an extremely long time, after events that I'm only able to paraphrase in extremely broad terms. With jadedness he couldn't conceal and also some measure of hesitation, my Narrator knocked on the door of this lengthy manuscript. A partnership of so many years can't just be terminated for the sake of vain pride. Everything else aside, whether we had liked it or not, we had both thought of new stories for one another during this long separation. A journey of brand-new sentences and possibilities must be undertaken so we could tend to our wounds. That's why we now harbor our disappointments along with all our sorrows and all that was left unuttered. We're like a pair of friends or lovers who, after having tried their luck at a myriad of different relationships, had no choice but to return to one another. Of course, this isn't the solution to a story, to some small adventure. Nor is there any sense, in these days that we're in, to say how, where, or with what sentence such a story began. Everything aside, there are some relationships one is increasingly less eager to understand or interpret to the fullest. In such circumstances I catch a glimpse of an old dream, imagining that after being witness to so much, we may just stake our own adventure between the parentheses of our silence that we're so well accustomed to. Perhaps that's simply what it is: the voicing of that longing in an entirely different form. I feel that it's worth trying—worth trying against all odds. To boot, there will be no revealing of a murderer or actual culprit at the end of the story; indeed, it won't even be apparent whether there was a murder or a crime at all. On this journey, your questions are all that you'll be asked to bring along. Take it as a subtle suggestion from a friend, so that you will always be vigilant, will not be so erroneous as to read this story before bedtime, and will not undermine another person in a way you may come to regret later.

I think you may also come across yourself, out of the blue, in this story. Discovering it, however, or choosing to mention it if the occasion should arise, is solely at your discretion.

3
An Inferno with Suad

IT WAS THEN THAT it was realized that the game couldn't be finished but could only be continued through different characters or words. It was doubtless a definitive moment, a moment that had been attempted, recounted, shared in one way or another, hopefully. In other words, what was at hand here was a story some were quite well acquainted with. Anything could set off memories of those old preparations and silences, just as anything could present the opportunity to relive those old bittersweet joys. Still, there were no easy answers. What stories, for instance, had such moments or phrases sparked once upon a time and, once that was determined, what turns of phrase, persons, or possibilities were within reach? Within the nuanced games of love, what sorrows were transferred from one to another, what yearnings made relatable and what joys shared? The Narrator wouldn't answer these questions, somehow avoided answering these questions, and contented himself with dwelling on his solitude, the value he gave to love and affection, and the paths he knew well; he focused on imagining all the noise around him dimming, even if briefly, in the face of all contradiction, the nuances in this sentence, and the misunderstandings. He then recalled all the stories in which his author had incarnated him as different characters and possibilities, thought to himself: it was rebellion, no matter how minor, to experience faraway climates with diverse people without telling anyone; a small rebellion that could give one a renewed zest for life, make it worth desiring despite all failures. Once, many years before, he had fashioned himself, for instance, as a librarian who had set out on a dangerous journey among books, who had never once returned from the places he'd gone, and hadn't wished to, a failed writer who had never written the book of his dreams. It was a hopeful inception that could enable the erasure or glossing over or, at the very least, concealment of shortcomings. As for silence, which could never be satisfyingly relayed to another, it would seep inevitably into the story. The moment would come, perhaps, that he'd be united with the poets, writers, images, words, and protagonists that had bestowed upon his life a myriad of different meanings and contributed, in one way or another, to his development. A moment, yes, only a moment. Yet would he be able to sufficiently relate and, more importantly, share that moment in one of the potential paths of the prolonged journey? There was a multitude of possibilities, after all, and each longing could evoke a defeat, each departure a return. There were many decampments toward another story; he'd travel by night, there would be motels, busses, restaurants of banishment and bathhouse smells, or it seemed likely that there would be: he'd casually converse with Franz Kafka in a language of solitude he loved so; during an expansive period of sleeplessness, he'd eat oysters with Baudelaire in Bucy-Saint-Liphard; he'd make love to a black woman in one of the hotels on Saint-Germain; he'd sip Assam tea with Virginia Woolf in a house in Bloomsbury one suppertime when Chekhov was also present; he'd discuss train stations with Anna Karenina; he'd meet Turgut Özben, though briefly, in the rundown diner of a rural town and tell him he wished to suggest a few additions to the Encyclopedia of the Disconnected[1]; *he'd explain to Ahmed Haşim why he was "accustomed to tedium," and try to lose himself with Suad in a piano melody or another inferno entirely; he'd introduce Alfred Jarry to rakı and go on a trip on the river with Rhoda. Afterward he would ask himself, however, what it was all for, when one was further estranged from his dreams with each passing day and failed to reach those he longed for—what was the point of postponing one's failures with such artifices? Then, at a time when everything seemed to devolve into an indelible conclusion, he'd attempt to fade into an apparition among all the books he so loved. An apparition, yes. It would be another form of leaving alone*

---

1   TN. A cult classic and cornerstone of Turkish literature, *Tutunamayanlar* by Oğuz Atay

those who ignored him to face their fears and their superficiality. He knew, after all, that the words were ready: for longing, resentments, the friends who were willing to be present on the other side of this story, for partners in crime and secret vindictiveness. When all was said and done, however, despite all hopes and good intentions, this story like the others before it was also unfinished, left incomplete by its author in a way that was evocative of so many relationships. Attempts that had started off as sketches and tapered off after a few sentences were too many to recount or even comprehend. Once, for instance, he was a stage actor who, having not been able to find his true character after having successfully played many roles in his extremely long career in theater (metaphors had had a significant part in that), anxious at not finding his true character and at the possibility of never finding it, never mind the hangovers or one's lonely early-morning regenerations or perhaps even because of them, these failures, committed suicide on stage during a suicide scene, only to have his committed audience applaud his throes of death. In another story he was a florist who prepared bouquets for breakups, whose door was often knocked on in the middle of the night by unex-pected guests, always welcome, for this very expertise he possessed; and in yet another a seasoned carpenter who sought an ancient love inside a painting, who dreamed of going on a voyage inside such a painting, whose poems smelled partly of aniseed, partly of sawdust, and partly of resin; who was also a collector of eyeglasses. Through these personifications his author had hoped to evade a curse, to relate the loneliness of those who were prisoner to little longings, only to have his attempts result in quiet disappointment—defeats, details, or small joys to be relived in a different sort of way each time. In other words, it was all the sum of possibilities and lives open to being shared at any time, and after a certain point, anything could be explained as a kind of preparation: a preparation for an adventure. Quandaries could be forgotten, and disappointments and defeats swept under the rug in favor of brand-new stories.

4
Waves, or the Pebbles of Max von Sydow

LATER I REACHED A twist in the road, a punctuation mark that I wasn't unaccustomed to, and I wished that an hour that I'd left behind in a sentence would alleviate an extremely protracted solitude. Then I thought to myself that I'd be able to continue that gloomy journey, someway advancing toward you or your shadow inside me, and I was reminded of the states of inebriation that weakened me and my desire to vanish inside those old books. I also thought, dolefully, of the storm, the minuscule havoc that no amount of words had been able to prepare me for. Against all hope, whether I wanted to or not, I advanced toward myself, only my own self. It was all as it used to be, as you see, it was all once more as it was in the days I had left behind somewhere. I then perceived that I was at a point of desperation once again, and said to myself, this is the most I can hope to enumerate or try to share with another; that was partly what gave meaning to my perilous journey within that dream or endless dark chimera. We had found each other, out of the blue, in a city whose people perplexed me more and more each day. I said, it should be noted, with slight embarrassment, "This place reminds me of a certain fear, of a northern harbor steeped in the smell of old ships, frozen seas, icebergs, and suns that never set." We were, at this point in the story, in a venerable restaurant on an immensely wide boulevard, a leftover from an ancient film. We each held a warm drink and I was struggling to tell you how the drink prepared one for new, silent, and inborn bereavements. You were smiling, saying, "I take it you like it here, I've been coming to this place for years," as though you sensed my timidity and all the things I wished to say but couldn't. You were taking my hands in yours, telling me that this song would never end, that it would also go on in others. People walked past, reminding us, or as though wanting to remind us, that there are relationships where one is merely a shadow. No one cared for another's sadness, what another felt and might communicate. It was then I came across Max von Sydow as he was in that old role of his. I said, "That movie might still be going on somewhere, still playing." The actors of our imaginations lived within us not as they were in real life but as the characters they played. It was the most important and indispensable rule of the game. To have passed over from that movie into this dream so abruptly was essential, inescapable, the merging of a person with his ghost. In such trysts everyone must play their own part, as well as the silence of that part, and the voyage to another, a completely different relationship in a completely different manner. "How long has it been the hour of the wolf?" I asked you then. You replied, "There are some apprehensions that can't be uttered and some emotions that can never be shared, but sooner or later, we come to resemble the person we're living with." I said, somewhat ashamedly, that I remembered these words from somewhere. You were then transformed into the specter of Liv Ullmann in the final frames of that one film. This terrified me. My terror turned you from one woman into another, then another, then another. Then all at once you attained the guise of that matchless song of voyage I remembered. "How did it all change so suddenly, at such an unexpected moment," I asked then, "how did we leave everything behind and get here?" Could it be a search, however hopeless, for an exit from a years-long and unforeseen imprisonment? At these words you seemed to withdraw back into your silence, with your gaze, unexpectedness, and your tendency to suddenly drift off, telling me, "I'm already there in your call, your never-ending story." At that moment I thought of all the possible meanings of the stories, and their associations in me, but I couldn't explain to myself where to put you inside this story, never mind what kind of story

it would be. In a familiar attempt at recovery, I merely said, "But
sooner or later you and I will disappear into the story, and no
one will know that we're here, never to return to our old lives,"
unable to say to my heart's desire, or even admit to myself, to be
perfectly honest, that in this case the words that carried me into
the sentence were left over from an ancient dream, a myth, so
to speak. This rhetoric changed the smile on your face, your eyes
warning me of a brand-new peril entirely. In reality I appeared
before my dream form once more with all the words I knew and
incessantly repeated for the sake of many a different rhetoric,
becoming the passenger of a separation, a hopelessness that I
had long been able to give meaning to. As such there were developments that were easy to sense, and oscillations between hope
and hopelessness that were easy to comprehend. To be a viewer,
a mere spectator to almost every relationship, to never mention
the obligatory standstill at a certain place, a near-impermeable
boundary, to appear as though you've never known such captivity, to never be able to say out loud that although there are
companionships that are quite easy for certain people, to people
forced to live like me they have always been loaded with compromise, diminution, and self-expulsion, to never be sufficiently
open with anyone, to consider such a thing a liability, postponing to ambiguity the dilemmas and obstacles a lover encounters—after all the disappointments and downfalls, did any of
this offer anything in the way of a solution? Where did that leave
me—in front of a crack in the door that made hope plausible
once again? Of course I could never ask you any of this, as just
then you were telling me that my companionship, my words,
were laden with irreplaceable warmth, that there was some pride
to be found in the fact that I had created you, produced you
from my imagination, without really knowing you, and that it
was time you faced this adventure, as well as—however briefly—
these people and this reckoning, omitting from your sentence,
however, the passion I had woven out of much shame and nour-
ished with many small joys. Roads already traveled doubtless

conveyed to me the reckonings that were long due, and the confrontations they brought with them. It was, after all, for the sake of examining such necessities that I had set out on this path. All said and done, however, the real challenge was sensing that this adventure was a pretext fabricated, invented for your journey toward another, to be able to endure the consequences of sensing it, and to be forced to relive the story. Yet it would also be ill-advised somehow to openly declare it, to try to share it. "You ought not to leave me alone in this completely unfamiliar city, whose people, language, and views I can't help but feel alien to; you ought to take me along on your journey," I then said. Near-collisions were, in a way, predestined in stories in which certain emotions were kept hidden. In reply, however, you merely smiled once more, telling me that I was downright naïve and inexperienced when it came to understanding such emotions. "But what about your longing for those small joys, your acquiescing to accompany me in this story, this dream?" I retorted. You countered that nothing was perfect and never would be. "This is an ancient delusion, used up years, even centuries ago," you said. "But now I have your return, the wait for your return, to deal with," I said. "I'll come back, of course I'll return," you interrupted, "this suffering must be dealt with no matter if one wishes to or not." I glimpsed then that your eyes had misted over slightly, wished that I could embrace you with all my might and all my weakness, my hopelessness and my self-deprecation. Yet I couldn't, I could do nothing. Max von Sydow materialized beside me once more, said: "The waves and the stones, the hour of the wolf draws near, and I must go to that shore." I can only react: "Now I know why you must go far away from here." You seemed to fade then, becoming translucent, your voice dimming, that scent of yours, which I could never describe, evaporating by degrees. I could understand or at least sense this story of hopelessness and I think that's partly why my eyes teared up a little. It was a story I knew well, that I lived inside of often, that I can't help but live inside. To live inside, yes, a lover or a passion, to imagine you had to or can despite any obstacle. Yet in time nothing is left behind, nothing remains except for the memories that return suddenly, the pang of self-deception, and the useless bouts of optimism. To have told me you'd return, to offer me your friendship as you always did in such circumstances, was in this sense disingenuous, an unburdening and a penance for a sin—if there was one. It was a small act of rebellion or a different form of reproach to evade my offer. For the first time in such a sentence, perhaps, it was the victim who had leverage. I open myself to dangerous allusions with some awareness of the fact. On the strange line between sleep and drowsiness it was completely unfamiliar images, perhaps, that would now receive me. "One day, perhaps, one day indeed," you said, smiling inwardly, "but know this, the hour of the wolf will always remain in our lives as a possibility, an irrevocability." The hour of the wolf, yes. These were the words that could bring tiny deaths into our present days. The sound of the waves crashing upon the shore drew nearer with each passing day.

There wasn't much to say, nor should there be, about this dream, the last chapters of which were designed, admittedly with some resentment, for our trip within the text. The only thing that remained was the magic of a question—simply a question—and its byproducts: had all the preparations been worth it, had we been united in that old and unfinished story, had we really inhabited that story, did it even exist for us, was it written?

This may have also been the reason that I would consider waking to a tedious Sunday morning on a bend in the road I'm no stranger to. I should remark that the silence I experienced this once in a silent house was one that was unfamiliar. I ought to also ask myself whether I could recount all this to another one day, in a completely different manuscript. I gave up, however, after a small about-face and an attempt at writing a sentence. In spite of all my efforts and good intentions, I'd never be able to answer the question the way I desired anyhow. Seeking refuge in reticence could, in this sense, offer a solution, a way toward hope.

For now everything around me seems calm as a millpond, ready to be filled with hope. In spite of the ugliness of the apartment blocks surrounding me, the rain is falling most prettily this evening. I now relive my invisibility on the balcony of this apartment I dropped by for the sake of a manuscript I believe I'll be able to write to its fullest someday. I tell myself that it's still lovely to be able to listen to and smell the rain, even after all the lives, poems, or songs, good and bad alike, and the stories indistinguishable from lies and deceptions. I perceive then the slightest scent of earth, and I feel like I should be able to share with you its evocations. Sharing an evocation, I murmur. Sharing an evocation. But it's through words, words, only words that you return here.

5
Hesitation

ALL SAID AND DONE, the tale appeared much changed, much more meaningful now. The Narrator was infused with the urgency of rebellion after this state he'd been forced to face for so many years, he could sense that he was in a place far from his author; that there were suggestions he could no longer consent to. The anticipated moment was here. There were re-emergences that couldn't be postponed.

6
Your Photograph toward Me

I WISHED TO TELL you that evening never to call me again, in the face of separation and abandonment, to keep up this passion and hopeless conversation; wished with unutterable longing that I could put into words the hell of postponing the joy of waking up together to another nebulous morning, advancing toward your fate one late night in a vastly empty street, and imagining making love and, out of nowhere, inserting you into it. I then thought of awaiting your return to these pages despite all my hopes, songs, and poetry, and it appeared that my only choice in this matter was to listen to only my own voice, for my own sake, while suffering perhaps that much more inside from my loneliness, your absence, this war. I was once more weathering the storm of a fresh attempt, the search for a shore, and a belatedness I knew very well by now. And yet I felt on the brink of walking toward you in that immemorial photograph of yours, didn't even want to consider that your persistent silence, indifference, and your refusal to come around here was an answer in and of itself. My journey within these words would always continue, in fact, while time flowed past; such sentences would remain in my life no matter if I wanted them to or not. Then there was the necessity that the old photograph, with all its evocations and reckonings, take its place in our history, our solitude. If you only knew how little hope I now harbor for an adventure of love that offers happiness. If you only knew the pain of diminishing a little more with each relationship. Doubtless I should have suspected this outcome in the very beginning, having experienced or been forced to experience the events of earlier texts, but what use is there in pointless bragging

and deceiving one another with so-called myriad experiences?
Don't we both know that despite all the suffering and the disappointments, we'll never be fully prepared for others? All said and
done, one doesn't easily recover from the trauma of the feeling
of insufficiency no matter how much credit we give ourselves for
these things we've endured. It was, in that sense, the death of
silence, unresponsiveness, and a dream that was chased for years
and reanimated against all sound judgment; it was an inner call
to me, to be perfectly honest, from the destruction you know so
well, the terrible dilemma of inadequacy; it was reminiscent of
the various deceptions of silence, the odor of old, age-old rains,
scenes of suicide and hospitals, unfinished tales, the unremitting
failure to coalesce with the city's women, smoking grass in the
streets without being able to pass out, and Sundays that awaited
solitude with poems that didn't wear their hearts on their sleeve,
that gave rise to new associations with each reading. I would set
out on an infinitesimal, mute voyage of solitude, the images of
a nightmare that constantly haunted me perambulating inside
me: I was in front of a mirror once more, struggling to alter my
skin, my hair, my appearance. In great agony I tore apart my
body and it was always the same body, it seemed, that kept resur-
facing from underneath. I appeared to be repeating, repeating,
repeating myself in spite of all my suffering and my hopes. In
those hours there was a terrible silence in the room—the room
I always strove to describe. On an inner breeze of other stories
and film stills I carried into this self-transcribing text certain
faraway sounds that could give it meaning or depth; such as the
sound of running water from a neighboring apartment, a door
creaking, or the clacking of a typewriter. In the nightmare I
stood in front of a mirror, yes, and despite all my words, with
great shame and hopelessness, I kept turning into myself without
ever making it to you.

7
Threshold

AND THAT WAS WHY it had all begun in the hope of a brand-new adventure, as though it were a brand-new game; a hope, a prospective love story or merely the illusion of passion. In that manuscript he'd once again envisaged becoming a completely different character to call to a faraway lover. After the mass of emotion weathered in the vague past, it would be easier to weave a togetherness out of words, to adapt it to his own ways. It would all begin with an appeal, and a string of words, hallucinations, and nightmares would determine the flow throughout the considerable length of the manuscript. Then he would endeavor, out of the blue and without his author's knowledge, to climb out of the manuscript, he'd proceed to seek her out, the elusive woman with extensive information about the works of his author. Would he be able to live out his independence in a restaurant, on a coast, or simply in the world, would a lover answer his sudden call? Then there was the question of whether he could explain to his author this journey, this compulsion for adventure. It was the first time such a thing had happened, after all, for him it all meant divulging to another a dream, a longing, an escape that was many years overdue. It should all be tantamount to the unexpected birth of an infinitesimal joy, of once again hoping for a passion or a lover. After dozens of experiences, however, it was a challenge to explain; after all, he knew from those old tales the fallaciousness of trying to impress a lover only with words. Yet at the end of the day it was a known fact that humankind was prisoner to tiny mistakes, often liable to pay for them in very costly ways. Resigning oneself to advancing within a dilemma, indeed, despite every known emotion. From here on, naturally, it would mean a wound would never heal, aching inwardly from time to time, a very well memorized story would be resumed no matter if one wished to or not. Yet weren't dreams often more cruel and dangerous than reality in their propitiousness and pretense of giving a reason to cling to life? In other words, was the author not even the tiniest bit right in assuming that we would never find the lover inside, and even if we did, never experience the passion that we wish for and seek, within another text?

8
Your Journeys after So Much Downpour

I NOW WISH TO speak to you about the magic of being able to get away once more from the city where I am, whether or not I want to be, condemned to live; wish to repeat my call to you, so familiar to you, from the shores of a different sea entirely; I want to regain my faith in this cry despite the residue of poetry left over from an illusion. Nothing but that lie transforms all our joys or allows our repetitive and ever-changing climates to perambulate within the sorrows of another. In other words, the only things that bring me closer to you are my misapprehensions and the words they trail behind. Yet despite it all I ought to track down a dream that will never end, I say to myself then. This must be the expression of our little deaths that constantly multiply in variety to tussle with us unexpectedly; the script that covertly pours the sorrow of the terrible adventure that is our sexuality that, despite all these dreams, we can't live to the fullest; or the ennui of an evocation dragged in by such-and-such a song. I understand then that demanding questions grow increasingly difficult to evade, telling myself that there's no point anymore in ignoring the consequences of this nightmare. Where, for instance, had I first dreamed it, what had prepared me for walking toward you after all this time? The attempt at removing myself from myself or, to be more accurate, that sliver of time that I was in and would rather not be in during the long and exhausting night trip I undertook to get here, under the pretense of resting my eyes because I was bored of the flickering, tenuous town lights in the train window that went past as I dreamed of fragments of entangled stories, or because I was sick of constantly being confronted with my own reflection? This moment of brief yet deep schism in which I nod off as I wait for a friend I hadn't seen for ages in this city, this little coffeehouse by the sea? A preamble whose words have long been forgotten, displaced? A night of inebriation that saw the forcing together of different incarnations of melancholy, a crowdedness, and the sudden reversals of death and joy? I can't know and cannot for the life of me explain the reasons for this indecisiveness, the non-responsiveness that stamps itself on my present more deeply with each passing day. To tell the truth, however, I think all four possibilities would've been fitting for the purposes of realizing this text. There was also an appeal to the matter that stemmed from the existence of stories that could be made possible by these choices. The author's indecisiveness, his at times apparent purposelessness within the choice of a pursuit was useful in that sense, as rare as that was. Yet when all was said and done, the accepted and prosaic progress of time in dreams had little meaning considering the likenesses of said dreams, which were secondary to the text. Each image could evoke another image, in that sense, just as each joy a season and each old street a rendezvous. Perhaps I had been able to go out into the district I grew up in on this throwaway evening of alcohol, timidity, and incomplete sex because I had unwittingly prepared for this small storm. I must have hoped to share, in this new attempt of mine, a word or simply a few details. The streets tasted of unequivocal sadness, no, even of exhaustion, and I seemed to have forgotten once more the path to your room, which I had never been to and would never be able to make out. Yet when I stumbled upon your shadow within my own self unexpectedly, without preparation, you stared me in the face as though I was a stranger and claimed not to know the person I was looking for, although you had been living around here for years. You took your leave almost immediately, too, smiling like in the moment of departure I had dreamed for you once. In reply to this attitude I could think of no hope, no nightcap, no tale of reunion. As in every passion, every relationship devolving into isolation, I had never been able to tell you what was on my mind anyway. The strange thing, however, was that this scene would repeat itself with only a few small details changed, that I'd keep running into you again and again and again on the way I assumed led to your room and you'd keep insisting that you didn't know "that woman." You would appear before me at times tetchy, at times affectionate, and at times indifferent. Perhaps it was only your plausibility that I wanted to assure myself of. Then all at once I found myself, unceremoniously, in introspection, a new rhetoric of muteness. It was one of the rooms I had wished to have you stop by, to wake up to a fresh morning with me; a room that smelled partly of suicide and partly of summer, in a house that had long fulfilled its place in my life. Right then, suddenly, a phone rang, ripping through the silence as it would have on a worn-out night, and I thought it must be you for sure, and this call was reminiscent of a return long awaited and worn out. My foresight was not incorrect: you were on the other end of the line. It didn't even cross my mind at that moment to ask you where you found this phone number, I was merely imbued with the longing for or the prospect of a singular story. For after the false hopes that had sprung from all those songs, films, and storms, you called me as though nothing had happened; as though we had never tried on for size other roles, lovers, and people within other manuscripts and sentences. I consequently told you that neither was I here and nor would I be—that I had died a short while ago. Indeed, I was telling you of a person who had died somewhere a short while ago, I was recounting in third-person singular the pang of being unable to return to myself, talking like it was someone else. A deep, long silence, reminiscent of estrangement, then entered our conversation. I felt you smiling and you said you recognized my voice, that this wasn't a nice game at all. Another silence, evocative of indecisiveness and regret, once again divided our conversation, and I said to myself that rain simply *must* fall during this brief conversation, that this sensation *must* be stirred in the minds of those listening to us or appearing to watch us. "He died two days ago," I said, in an attempt at resuming this awkward conversation, "it's normal for you to liken my voice to his, because I'm his twin, and as for his never having mentioned me to you, I'm not surprised, because we were never fond of one another, we simply couldn't be; after a certain point all we were was the other's shame, plausibility, mirror image, and accountability, and that was why we thought of going away to different climates to try being completely different people," I continued, as though to exact some small revenge for something I couldn't define or that avoided definition. The rest was the extension of an awfully familiar ploy: I'd have to endeavor a brand-new loneliness, I had arrived here under the influence of a foresight, one that was rather difficult to explain. I would return to that faraway country very soon. There beside me, however, was a notebook, and in the notebook the residue of words that had gone unshared in spite of all hope: "It appears my twin dropped by your neighborhood in the early afternoon when he first sensed he would die. There was a detail, a last detail it seems, that he wished to share with you. The notes left to me don't explain what it could be. But I'm told that you inexplicably kept appearing before him under different guises that evening, insisting that you recognized neither him nor the woman in question. This is what I can make out of the depiction of a dream that he jotted down in the last pages of this book. Here, also, in between a pair of tiny and tenuous parentheses, it's indicated that these words were written for you, and only you. That's why I awaited your call and hoped to meet as soon as possible, for no reason save delivering this notebook to its owner binds me to this place." Words, words, words. Another silence around that point divided our conversation. "Now you understand the secret to the game, but I'm sorry for you that you had to suffer so much and so unnecessarily for your useless, obstinate plea," you said, adding, "I'll come again, I'll come for sure." The night fell on these sentences with all its indifference. The park where I once dreamed of meeting with you must still be in a season of melancholy and loneliness. Perhaps it was evening and a man sat there on a bench, not really knowing where or which home to go to. Then abruptly there was the sound of footsteps on dry leaves, fast approaching, heading toward a manuscript. Fear, loneliness, and footsteps, yes. Could it be that it was all from another story that strained to make itself told? I couldn't say. I didn't feel like saying, didn't feel like answering or even remembering. I seemed to be living an entirely new sense of loss and estrangement in the night. And that was why I thought that maybe, with your lover someplace far away from this coffeehouse, this shore, and this dream, you may be able to start a morning, a journey, or merely a sentence of affection anew.

9
Silence

DID THIS MEAN THAT *the only things left behind were the desire to recount a passion, a dream, or dejection, or to share sorrow with another, or the effort to understand or describe a lover based on various clues? The question warranted, of course, arriving at different answers, phrases, or ambiguous parentheses. Yet after the loss of so many songs, so many persons' failure to come back and so much poetry left unwritten, to tell the truth, such questions tended to lose their meaning. And after all, belated comprehensions would, as though to confirm the stories, never be mentioned, would be accepted in resigned silence, to never be examined again. Everyone was aware of their part in the crime, or would be. Besides, there was no need or viable excuse to turn these texts, these effusions, into a story in its own right. Still, there was something about this adventure that wasn't working, that strained to be told but couldn't be . . . it was an old, an age-old longing.*

10
The Arab's Coffeehouse, Shores, Train Whistles

THE ARAB'S COFFEEHOUSE IS overrun this morning with those who fail to write what they wish, who inhabit a dream. It's a sentence that appears evocative, seems to express hurt and exasperation; a sentence that's bound to be associated with the magic of certain words and reminiscent of those old illusion-laden photographs. We could also call it, perhaps, a beginning that engenders hope in the way of conveying and sharing a game that has long been reckoned with or an attempt at self-examination. A little hopeful attempt, yes. Yet despite all the discourse, imagery, and insufficiently expressed parentheses I can't help but carry within me, I honestly still don't understand my impulse to call this coffeehouse, which I may have passed by before in another lifetime of loneliness infused with completely different words, the Arab's Coffeehouse, just as I don't understand my effort to live by discounting certain truths and longing, within this text, for another story. Is it that I'm attempting to pursue once more a presentation of previous lives along with the evocations such names are sure to bring? Maybe. As a matter of fact, considering the stately trees surrounding it, this place could just as easily be called the Fig's Shade, or that of the chestnut, or walnut. As for the real name of the coffeehouse, it must be a lot uglier than any number of my guesses. Then one is faced with the magical bittersweet joy that stems from not knowing certain things, or at times refusing to know. We could say that it's a small act of rebellion, or a bid to delay a quite possible defeat. If you only knew, for instance, how marvelous and soothing it is to be unable to tell which lives you're sharing, with whom, and in what manuscript, fancy, or sentence; to consider that I may

have lost something in a story, and to have created every sorrow
and joy in my dream in this attempt at a new appeal. This is
perhaps the apex of this bizarre adventure that revolves around
you; the unavoidable activation of a self-defense mechanism one
could become attached to *ad finem*, the need to flee, as much
as possible, from an obligation that has long been defined. Yet
I'm no longer as ashamed of these exercises in self-deception
as I used to be, for I have many ways to detect the things that
await me at some point down the road. Perhaps the many years
and my extensive and strenuous trips among manuscripts were
necessary to find out what minutiae those who'd achieved certain lives avoided bearing. For one to learn to bear one's own
selfhood, shortcomings, and contrarieties, however, hazarding
such expulsions was already obligatory. Making do with self-an-
swering questions is much easier and bearable in that regard.
How many of us are given so many reasons to ask whether
these delusions befell us while in stolen and deceptive states of
inebriation, how many of us say it, how many of us refuse their
enchantment? More importantly, contrary to initial assumptions, did these minute and thrilling games not bind us more
firmly to life? Can I not assess my willingness to bury within
me the nuance I unexpectedly discovered tonight in this coffeehouse, my longing to forget the role I've assumed nowadays,
even if for a while, and abscond to one of those old, lost fancies,
my ability to remember that peerless sea scent once more despite
the vague toot of a train whistle, as my struggle to love this city
that drifts farther away from me with each passing day, with its
bridges built every day but in turn also torn down? Can a similar
struggle not be found within a person who stays indifferent to
my existence and my appeals? It's like us, after all, to be melancholy, to turn autumnal, to revel in bus trips in the middle of the
night, in a motel somewhere between two forsaken towns, in the
wrenching pain and poetry of the tawdry meals in the tawdry
restaurant of that motel; it all becomes those people who, like us,
are forced to remain in the beginning, talking to their shadows,

unable to belong anywhere in spite of all their wishes. The Arab's Coffeehouse is very becoming on this cool summer morning, yes. I know very well now which stops the train that's now in the station will make next, the games it will host, and with which actors. Idealtepe, Süreyya Beach, Pendik. The people who were once alien to this city, whose stories I shared in their myriad forms, have now departed to locations far away. Irreconcilably different departures in irreconcilably different countries and vernaculars await them now, as well as irreconcilably different reunions. Pendik, Süreyya Beach, Idealtepe. The scent of the sea and its evocations. Never mind, never mind, push past it, push past it, as an old friend would have said. New inquests will bring us nowhere, and another attempt at trying to get past the hopelessness is tantamount to rowing upstream, now. After all, most if not all those who experienced those spaces know very well what we lost even in the very recent past. Considering it all from this perspective, it may be for the best to leave everyone alone with his own stories and evocations. I suppose it must be something not unlike awaiting a familiar sound, some fecundity, or remorse that may give way to joy, to rise from an ostensibly unresponsive street. Let's see to what familiar beach or crack in the door this longing will bring us. I considered once more, for example, those who'll one day be able to hear us and these things we've endured in the way we want to be heard. The possibilities were oftentimes uplifting and just as often anxiety-inducing. At the end of the day, in such efforts of conferring, no risk is too great to turn away from. It's an old, old tale, in other words, a journey that in our eyes alluringly, almost irresistibly paints this adventure. The allure of heading into danger, yes. I hope that one day, after a long time has passed, after the numerous layers of this story have been lived out and, most importantly, rewritten by others, I'll be able to talk to you of remaining grievances. For now, though, only dreams, designs, and little anticipations. Hopes that bind us to one another, to stations that we may happen upon at inopportune times and in lost motels. It's then that I say to myself, now is the time to wait somewhere, small suitcase in hand, between a few lines, or in some sentence that may have gone ignored. Many reasons for travel and small joys have accumulated inside you. You recall the poetry of certain sounds and wish you could relive what you've lost. You have been told, also, that you're living in memories, in the dream of a lover that never changes. Then you think of defeat and the lovemaking left inside the dreams, and you strive to forget yourself once more, to look the other way.

11
The Earthquake Inside

As it was, must he now undertake a new complicity, despite all his resentments, with an author who seemed capable of dreaming up new stories based on certain bodies of text or dubious cues, making all the arrangements necessary for such preparations, consciously ignoring the parts he didn't see fit to include and striving to tell any lie necessary to ensure the persuasiveness of events, or set out on another road afresh, toward another person, another hell or author? A ripe search for an unexpected story, untested possibilities, he thought elatedly, remembering, all of a sudden, the same old stories, the images, and the regrets. Yet he'd attempted this adventure, these emotions and sentiments before. That was partly the reason for the blizzard of anxiety and unavoidable and inevitable questions that overtook him. Could one be sure, for instance, where a relationship, a love adventure, and, increasingly, a story would begin and end? Could a lover not keep going, in spite of all the years and changing seasons and yearnings alike, within another, silently if need be? Most importantly, would these departures and obligatory reunions ever be spent, our journey to our brokenness or to our choices ever end?

12
The Chinese Restaurant

SO NOW ONCE AGAIN I find myself at the same dead end or awakening. A familiar gloom descends upon me and I think of the songs, the intoxications that are identical to escape, the summer clothes that are kept waiting in mourning, endless mourning, forgotten Four O'Clocks wilting somewhere. I also dream of the icy scent of aniseed, it half-scares and half-revolts me. Perhaps that's why I think that every person dies a different way in each relationship, is spent in a different way. Something shakes me to the core, something I still can't seem to name collapses once more in our tiny, quiet lives woven out of isolation. I want to tell myself once more, no matter how hard it is, that you won't be returning to this manuscript, this story that gives no clues as to when it will be written. Consequently I'm reborn into a certain sorrow, dreaming of the scent of September, thinking that possibilities are endless and will surely give us fresh games to exist within, but still apprehensive about being confronted with my questions and my lack of answers. Where was the original error, for instance, the actual error that brought me, us, here? In my likening you, always, to poetry, or sanctuary, or desolation? Or the fact that I had lost my way, once again, in this lengthy text, or my excessive pushing of boundaries or my becoming besotted, once again, with being a hero, a self-professed charmer? Was there nothing wrong with this picture, and if not, should it all be seen as the natural, unavoidable result of a passion condemned to remain unfulfilled? There was a time when the effort to answer this last question could have taken me to another dead end, forced me to hazard one of those little storms once more, whether I wished to or not. But it's too late for that now. To be more accurate, certain experiences assure me that similar lines of questioning won't take me anywhere. How, then, can I explain this effort, the hope that has sprung to life within me just because? Why do I think of these words, why undertake directing this hopeless tirade at you? In hopes of getting over or turning a blind eye to certain conundrums to discover a new smile for myself or a completely new, unexpected crowd? To be able to picture once more, on a rainy night, that crack in the door? To stand in front of that door, on that threshold, and hope for sudden rebirth? None of these things, to be completely honest. After all, I made up my mind many years ago that maintaining futile longings is pointless. Yet still ultimately it feels as though there are things I haven't been able to tell you in spite of all the paroxysms, preparations, and exercises in loneliness, as though I were forever appearing before you lacking, in spite of all the lies I know. And it isn't as if I'm unaware of the importance of shortcomings in love, in all human relationships. All said and done, however, one can't readily accept, after all of one's lifetimes, one's constant tardiness, especially that which manifests in a relationship, one's timidity when cracking open a door, or empty wineglasses on a lonely evening, or believe one keeps on carrying a constantly repeating cycle of regrets from one relationship to the next. The only things left behind are the fallacies. At that point I try to derive some small joy from the burden of our relationship, causing it to remain a beginning, a possibility, an unfulfilled longing. For we both know extremely well how even prolonged, domestic relationships wear out eventually, despite the best intentions, and lose their initial luster. So it seems our attachment is destined for brilliance because it will never give way to that kind of isolation or unraveling. We'll never find the opportunity to binge on one another, for instance; I'll never become well acquainted enough with your body, with your quotidian and most natural habits to feel the urge at some point to leave you for the sake of an ambiguous, likely unwise longing. You'll always remain for me a probability, a choice tantamount to long unexpected journeys. I will always remember you as you are in these sentences, even after the passing of many years, sentences, and joys. Perhaps this is the crack in the door I've mentioned before. On this earth where almost every single gesture is contrived in a silent game, where desperation is constantly masked by new discoveries of words and fashions, all in service of maintaining a system, of which the meaning has never really been determined, and humanity's great bliss and principles, the near-complete loss of which is accepted by only a scant few, is it not incomparably elating to be able to revel in such detail, with all the sentiments, commentary, and evocations, despite the horrendous pain of self-reflection? Are the pain and defeat's detritus not preferable to having never experienced the turmoil and anxiety of preparing for a new lover? You make no reply to these questions, and I know you might never be able to, but your silence won't stop me from multiplying alongside you within other stories. Whatever experiences and yearnings may come to pass, a passion is always one's unbroken progress toward oneself and one's dream, no matter the circumstances, it's impossible not to carry something from one relationship to the next. After that point, you may be able to bring once more to your life's agenda the questions you had been putting off for so long. Did we go on an adventure in between the lines, for instance, accompanied by several glasses of wine, or seek refuge between a pair of parentheses, clandestinely, and however briefly? Did that waiter with excellent manners at the Chinese restaurant recognize us both, and would he recognize us again, on one of the nights we'd go there, as the entirely unconnected protagonists of entirely different stories? In time, could we come to love the matchless alliance of red and black? Or was everything in this game synonymous with a lie, as it was often wont to be—did you just stick your head in the door, leaving me to choose living with that dream and resentment? Had we been able to tell each other that everything, in time, would turn into a sum of symbols, a shared isolation, increasingly a delusion?

Would you and I one day be able to talk about the secret of those shards of glass? For this game to seem like it was played by the same rules as the others, prolonging itself with renewed questions, did that explain enough?

13
A Summer's Evening in Sintra

QUESTIONS, QUESTIONS, QUESTIONS. PERHAPS one could never hope to escape the obligation to experience new words, seasons, or persons in the name of a compulsively gripping, belated story. As a narrator, he once more nervously considered his role in such a dream; the covert agreements he'd made with certain protagonists, the unfinished, unrealized designs, and the lies that had never taken anyone anywhere in the history of this long body of text. He made coffee on the stove and checked that he had enough cognac and tobacco, wishing inwardly that he could tell someone about the magic of withdrawing into the night, of seeking sanctuary there after a barrage of songs. These were actually among the details and themes his author also frequently returned to and for some reason enjoyed repeating. Such nights contained unspent sentences and words that invited certain memories and sorrows; such nights meant a journey, belated and oft-unrealized, to a person, a story, or a far, extremely faraway country. (He was no stranger to such sentiments, of course, or to similar turns of phrase, considering the adventures he'd previously experienced or had to endure. He was a prisoner to certain obsessions, he was aware his author had introduced him as such, a prisoner to certain obsessions. The trouble here stemmed from the fact that as with almost all matters and sentiments, there was a hyperawareness concerning certain truths. As it was, however, hopelessness tended to knock on our doors at unexpected times in unexpected forms. One could never know their location on the path to transformation and self-reflection, and could never hope to know. The pain of wisdom, however, had been mentioned many, many centuries ago.) That's part of the reason why I must devise a completely different history and if necessary an appearance, some sort of mask, he thought to himself, so I can enjoy certain longings and bittersweet joys, and that was partly why he didn't condemn this groundwork, was not disconcerted by this sentiment, the ancient longing in that phrase. Yet against all hope, in the room where he'd come to live in different texts in the name of utterly disparate resentments, he found his reflection in the mirror anxiety-inducing and even downright frightening. He would have liked to speak of his age, of his elderliness, but was not able. Then he tried to smile once again, remembering that for years he'd chased the same theme and the same poem and had sought sanctuary in the same smiles or treacherous joys; imagining himself once more on a departure, some small beginning, a story left half-finished. A melancholy summer's evening, for instance, was transpiring in Sintra just now, and he was the passionate protagonist of an unpredictable path in a faraway land. In the story he'd pictured possibly having dinner in this tiny city, on an evening like this, with the mysterious woman he had once glimpsed on the Salamanca–Lisbon train, whose image he'd kept to himself in spite of all the years that had passed since. The calm fragrance of an all-too-familiar loneliness and an unparalleled plant life seemed to abruptly descend upon his surroundings. The dreamlike person before him was in fact his own reflection, or illusion, or even his defeat. It was a game of minutiae: a game that could be played and interpreted in different ways depending on the varying flow of time. Now, for example, they spoke to one another of distant climates, the moods and resentments that had engendered them and that they'd soon return to, merging into one another in an aged, full-bodied intoxication, rediscovering wine and music as though they had never parted ways, dreaming of losing themselves anew in an instant of eternity. Wine and music indeed. That may have been the evening that he was introduced to the incomparable despondency of Fado. "Amalia Rodrigues," said the waiter, leaning close, "Amalia Rodrigues; from this moment on you shall never forget this voice." Amalia Rodrigues was with him now, years after the melancholy summer's evening during which that story had transpired. With him now in the form of a sentence, in his room, his loneliness, his pain, and all his longings for former lovers; as a friend that had always kept him company, as a fancy that some might find preposterous, a myth, or even just a possibility. He would return to Lisbon that evening still in thrall to this unexpected discovery, search for the Lisbon of his dreams again in this city whose language he'd found impenetrable, and haul his defeats, self-deceptions, the regret of dinners never held, and the rules of the game once more to a decrepit and shoddy hotel room. He would then nurture the remorse of having come here on this summer's evening on his own, thinking of the loners who simply could not unite, the desperate ones who doggedly pursued unattainable dreams. On several ensuing evenings after that, he had sat in the same spot in a coffeehouse whose name he couldn't quite recall nowadays. He'd met a fantastically old waiter then; in the face of the disparate realms of language where they had attained their full personalities, they had conversed of even the most abstract subjects they could dream up or longed to discuss. In the later hours of the night they had a few drinks together and talked of memory-laden bed-and-boards, incompatible sexuality and the pain it often brings, the obstructions in the way of sharing it, the books unfinished, a matter not helped by being imprisoned in a city. Everything rang of Fado at the time: melancholy, without narrative, without hope of return. Then, wandering through the timeworn streets of Lisbon, he'd felt the pangs of an otherworldly story making itself felt inside him. The story of a waiter dying an extremely prolonged death between a shoddy bed-and-board and a coffeehouse, he said to himself. He was absolutely sure that someday he'd tell his author about this reverie.

14
Your Face, Left to Me

BECAUSE MY ENTIRE CONSCIOUSNESS then seems to be gripped by heat, a bizarre kind of heat. I promptly light up a cigarette, and despite feeling somewhat wearied and somewhat embarrassed, I say: at least we're in an antechamber of love with no one able to see us; we belong to one another. Then I sense that you can't hear me, cannot even see me. I shake myself out of inertia. I think of your face left to me, your body I couldn't indulge in, your door I could not knock on. For every detail I'm forced to live out, am practically obliged to live out, lives on in you, proliferates in you, breathes with you. Out of the blue I think of a placid, supremely quiet island shore, its sea urchins, mussels you can fry in a tin, the rum taverns I never had the chance to really enjoy, the fatigued lurching of a darkly well-dressed and ancient woman down a wide, noisy avenue, the reek of mackerel, Jewish homes preparing for Passover, the story of leek dumplings, the night buses along the Bosphorus, the days dawning with the horns of ferries, Efrahim and Selami, Agia Paraskevi Day, the sounds of the lute, the piano, and the qanun, September in a waterfront mansion on the Bosphorus and Suad prolonged within me, the foulness and beauty of the streets of Şişli, the extraordinary singularity of the terrain that is Istanbul; I recall paradoxes and deferrals. It's then that an ancient and not at all unfamiliar question arises in my mind: was it you I had loved, or the shadow of a possibility that had trailed me for years? In such a place all I could do was count minutes, only the minutes. You then appeared before me in a vestibule, in the form of a vanishing dream. I found myself wandering in the hallways of a hotel soaked in the smells of alcohol, avoidance,

and loneliness, its history written in the dead night of silence.
Once again I was reticent about encountering mirrors, ashamed
once more of being always a prisoner to words and only words.
What hallway is this, I asked myself, what room were we in just
now? My gaze fixed once more on one of the mirrors. I expected
that despite my inner storms I'd never receive a response from
my reflection, and I won't lie, I was rather frightened of it. It was
as though I was bringing myself news of a looming threat, my
impending death inside a lover. I was at a point in time difficult
to determine. Had I just now emerged from this love adventure,
or many, many years ago? What reflection of evasion, muteness,
or nighttime did I see before me now? Stories and shattered
mirrors. I've never forgotten this trope and ought never to, I said
to myself then, and you seemed to consider my words to be a
sort of secret pact. You waited for me at the end of the hallway
in one of the dresses I had thought of buying for you, that I
had pictured you wearing. My very essence was overtaken by a
shudder as you said, "Christian Lacroix," appearing to remember
this small detail, and continued, "Thank you so much for everything. But if you had only been able to push aside those words
and stories and come to me." Your words seemed to contain
some sort of enchantment, an enchantment that's like suddenly
finding yourself lost on a strange street, the abrupt discovery of
a courtyard, which you're then somehow unable to exit. Once
more you were at a remove open to brand-new shadows, memories, and questions. In turn I asked how we were to change this
time difference between us, and how had you suddenly entered
this story at a time I least expected? "All is not as it seems, only
as it wishes to be seen," you replied, as though you had foreseen
this question that I simply couldn't bring myself to ask, and
added, "Let's go, let's go. Where I'm taking you, you'll set out
for completely different words and songs. An incense burns now
in my room, one you'll recall from an old, a very old story."
In that heated moment, suspended for eternity, I once again
contemplated, for some reason, meeting with you in a secluded

hotel in a town whose name I'd never be able to know or discover. Then we made love on silky sheets on an enormous bed. I glimpsed your back and haunches, your nakedness reflected off of the mirrors around us, as the strange smell of the incense burned in my nostrils. I ran my lips and tongue over your body and you in turn pulled my swelling member between your legs, saying, "You must flow into me, melt inside me." Now, I said, we disappear inside our dream, permeate one another. The smell of incense burned my nostrils and it felt as though this was my first journey to passion, to a lover.

15
The Old Geography of Solitude

In other words, that evening had been the threshold of a brand-new story, a hope, once more. As it was in many journeys to a place or a person, however, the story would also remain within a dream, to be brought to another relationship with a measure of bitterness and apprehension. Such evenings had actually taken place before. The difference was the strong illusion of experience and a bold progress toward an imaginary lover with no thought for the risk of a greater hopelessness. Doubtless this attempt at a relationship would be longer lasting, drastic, and crushing. But what was the limit of defeat, the return to inadequacy, and most importantly, this timeline we were on? Where, on what geography of solitude, had this relationship occurred? Would they one day come to live on that distant island dreamed up by his lover that he wished to create even despite a few little lies, and wander, filled with new longing, on the verge of such a room? All else aside, who was the lover, how would she be defined one day, described? At what point in this exhausting journey did he stand, where would he head from here, how, and diminished by how much? These may well have been questions that needed answering, questions that could be prolonged, as previously, through certain possibilities and ambiguities, that could contribute in some way or other to the conception of a story. Ambiguities and crumbs of hope, yes. Did these words signal the possible discovery, at an unexpected time, of a desperately sought way out?

16
Walking in a Mirror

I'M ASSUMING TONIGHT THAT you could stand once more in front of the mirror for me. It's an image that's essential for me to follow the tracks of a fresh delusion, a theme I assumed I'd be unable to exhaust so easily, and this adventure that I undertook despite being aware of all its consequences, indispensable, so to speak, for tiny deaths and hushed rites of burial. Each affair is a new sorrow, every passion in some way the same as death, after all. I then imagine the room where you stand in front of the mirror as being in that house on the beach, recollecting once again the sound of the waves upon the shore and the vastness of the sea. I'm haunted then by the shadow of a lost lover on a summer's evening. Let us imagine, for instance, that the scent of the sea has suffused our skin, and we've returned to this house from the beach or a sun-soaked boat trip. All day long we've gazed at one another, desired one another only with our eyes, and talked of the stories and people we've been forced to experience, and of lovemaking magnified by imagination. We can hear the sound of the waves from behind the curtains, the open window nudging the curtain aside slightly. We prolong our lovemaking as much as possible, I enter you again and again, then we smoke a cigarette or two. Tonight, however, it's a bit different, tonight you must be filled with the apprehension of the imminent tomorrow, you must appear to yourself partly giddy and partly hopeful. For you're about to head into the story of a predictable rainstorm, to another lover. You'll shiver slightly as the loves you leave behind become your future misgivings. In front of that mirror, you'll be taken over by the enchantment of a call that's not at all unfamiliar to you. It's at such a time that

I'll want to reach out to you, keeping to myself my part of our story without extending to you any resentment or shortcoming. With my dreams, words, and myriad possibilities I'll lure you back behind the mirror, I'll tell you that to merely reach out your hand, take a tiny step, will suffice for you to find me. You'll look at yourself once more, at your long red hair, blue eyes, and full lips, and say, "Words, words, words." Knowing your reflection in the mirror to be equal to my call will in you, perhaps, become the expression of regret or an unanticipated solitude. You'll raise your finger to your lips, wish to say something to yourself as you think of my presence in the room. Then, exactly at that moment, you'll be thoroughly gripped by a new trepidation as you realize that this game had been played before, at an utterly different time and in a completely different story. You'll ask then if you can live to the fullest this prohibited zone, or this shared isolation, as you try to grasp the point in the story at which you were forced to enter this body of text. "As it turns out, it was all wrong from the beginning," you'll perhaps say, "I was never in that house or that relationship, haven't traversed those sentences and phrases for so long, and he only produced me from his imagination." Producing a lover in one's imagination, luring her out of it . . . yet I had always been right there in front of you, I was with you along with your silence and all your evasions during your brief journey in the mirror. My remorse in the mirror was in part my own defeat, your evasion my appeal, your indifference my call. Producing a lover in one's imagination, loving her thus, appealing to a passion by engendering it in the imagination. I once more thought of many questions and solitudes wavering around this bizarre phrase, always being reminded of old loves, dispassion, abandonments, undesired separations, and the smell of whorehouses, and I thought, what affair, what lover, what tiny joy is there that isn't born in one imagination and spent in another? Then I felt slightly ashamed of myself, not to mention exasperated, recalling the enormous quantities of time I wasted on nuance and these useless, impractical words. There were times such as these when I go silent, without mentioning anything to anyone, and try to hide between a pair of parentheses or between lines. My occasional surfacing to look for you in these journeys between texts could only be explained by my reluctance to abandon this particular story. And that's partly the reason that we're here among these prolonged phrases this evening. On two very disparate sides of the mirror, we search once more for a theme I expect never to be able to exhaust. And I can't say why, but once again I'd like to bring to this text all the candlelights of my past, all its incense, cheese, and soup aromas, a walk on a rainy Sunday, frost-covered benches and piping hot coffee on a nighttime beach. The infamous mirror reappears, however, and I must assume my real role in the play once again. You apply some lipstick to your lips, as well as some joy and a bit of jadedness. Whether I'd like to or not, I can hear knocking on the door. I assume my role in the play, indeed, and assume that I can set out on the search for a completely different text with a brand-new sentence.

17
A Song with Amalia

Now Amalia Rodrigues continued to sing that song of melancholy. His coffee had gone cold, he had only a few cigarettes until dawn. At that moment, he fostered the joy of being able to wake once more, and even more strongly than before, to the invitation of words. His masks, costumes, fantasies, allusions, dead ends, obsessions, punctuation, all that he hid in parentheses and between lines, all were ready once more. The game continued one way or another, in other words, it would inch along, however slowly, to wherever it was headed. He would try to relate this sentiment to his author as soon as he could. He would attempt to verbalize this sentiment, this surrender, his obligation to live, despite their many differences in opinion and life experiences. Imagining that, for his author, he was only a possibility beyond all familiar approaches, would lend this story a completely different meaning. After all, they both knew that they had merged together unexpectedly in the name of a silently established solidarity. Because of that, perhaps, it would be easier to bear this new journey. The habitat was open, should be open, to those willing to listen to it for better or for worse, to put it another way. That was a necessary belief, an inevitability as well, to ensure the continuation of the journey in the face of any and all delusions. That he was dreaming of a balmy, warming breeze on such an evening, that he was setting out on a brand-new voyage in the name of the possible lives on this island, with its flickering lights in the window of his room, were these things not the most telling proof?

18
Melancholy, the Qanun, Afternoon, and Other Such Things

STRICTLY SPEAKING, WE HAD always existed. We had lived within one another's storm whether we wished to or not, we had been tangling together with all our avoidances, shortfalls, habitual defeats, our predisposition to introversion, our departures and silences, for a long, long time. It was only our sentences that differed, at most, our words, cataclysms and melancholies, perhaps. When that was the case we blamed only our own selves for our solitude, and I found myself almost happening upon your trail when I least expected it. Was this a delusion, an ancient deception, I wonder? Yet whatever our experiences and reasons for parting, we couldn't find easy respite from one another despite our parentheses and the punctuation marks that could at times provide rest or sanctuary, our longings in the name of possibility and unending passion becoming instead an obstacle, unreachability. For different stories and sentences often got involved and, as mentioned at some point or another, different melancholies merged with different stories. Different stories and melancholies, yes. At such times, everything seemed like an afternoon or some such thing, rang of solitude and muteness. I never tired of recounting such afternoons, thus never tired of experiencing them. Only, in those hours, I thought of old turns of phrase, thought I glimpsed your shadow or your fragrance in the depiction of a street. I then imagined you as a red-haired, pale-skinned, blue-eyed lover. There were times I claimed to be setting out in search of a manuscript. It was meaningful, of course, this departure, formidable. Then it was afternoon or some such thing, yes, something like afternoon, for the depiction of unwritten passions and unlived lovemaking and intoxications. I reach this manuscript now as a new exile, as the protagonist of a story who hasn't found where he belongs despite all his explorations and attempts. And to be perfectly honest, for the life of me I can't understand what manuscript this is, or what game. Our estrangement continues, proliferates on its own terms. With bittersweet joy I set out once more toward sentences I'll try in new configurations in every story, rather tentatively withdrawing into that obscure sense of deficiency.

19
You Were Prisoners to Deception

HE WAS NO STRANGER to this story, naturally, but there were countless benefits to be had from revealing the truth and repeating it incessantly for the sake of prolonging the story in some way. It wouldn't be his first time, for instance, falling prey to various deceptions on his voyage to passion; it wasn't his idea to suddenly renew his hopes or let himself be enraptured by a lover in hopes of a new life, whereas the longing to lure a lover, through words alone, to a life and a passion could only be credited to the depiction of an ancient and oft-incarnated desperation. He knew this story, he'd lived it. What was it then that he so sorely hoped would be expressed, shared, spun into a story? Words? The words that had their own special history and implications in each and every person? The search for a rhetoric itself, or its unfussy coming into being? Resentment at the continued failure to make a dream heard? Some "thing" that can't be described or defined, that remains incomplete despite all efforts, despite the constant pursuit of this "thing"? All of these possibilities were acceptable, to be fair, all could very well be worthy of consideration. All said and done, there still remained a question that at this point needed answering, or at the very least asking and probing. That was the difficult part: relating it to another and resigning oneself to living with the implications of this question.

20
Cognac Glasses on the Beach

NOW IT APPEARS AS THOUGH I must return to a story I abandoned many, many years ago. On a newly encountered beach, just before an impending storm, a downpour, a picture of happiness, I ask myself whether to allow myself hope once more in spite of all my hesitation, recalling the midnight phone calls prompted by solitude, the regrets, the defeats woven of misplaced joy, and suggestions, suggestions, suggestions. I want to know whether I can find joy in an evening after all the people, if I will one day return to that Jewish neighborhood and find those people, the people who have scattered, were forced to scatter, all over the globe, on an unexpected street, whether I'll want to somersault in the streets after such an evening affords a night of intoxication, what suit I should pick for which poem, with which smile and presence I should stand before you, what trains or buses I ought to take, and what sentences will serve me as an escape or a sanctuary. We may now be at an extremely special point in a passion we can experience quite clandestinely, through a story or a handful of ambiguous words, and the effort to change a manuscript, a life, together, after having waited for so long. For it's as if I heard or sensed that you entered this story from someplace I don't know and can't define; I can more or less understand, even though I can't see you or pervade you as much as I'd like to. So the game is replayed once more. And if we're indeed prisoners to such delusions, if we must be in the midst of such melancholy, then I say that this game must never end, and this wine be drunk with this dinner, this isolation multiplied, this bizarre monologue count as a dialogue, and this prolonged death left in abeyance. In truth, I can't say I don't sense any obstacles to this rendezvous. That is to say, I can more or less discern the impossibility of casually losing ourselves in this long-awaited and pictured story, despite my intense longing, or that after a small spark of bliss we'll invariably find ourselves at the same place, the same dead end. The first hours of an affair . . . I had said to myself once that I should always keep separation in mind. I still believe in the relevance of that fear, to be honest. Yet as you'll well recall from those old texts, deferrals laid at another's door or imputed dilemmas, one cannot easily stop pinning one's hopes on oneself. In that sense you're no lover showing up on my doorstep unexpectedly but rather the indeterminately situated protagonist of this story I'm struggling to place. It's as though only I dream up and design your choice of words, your smile, the way you gaze at me, and every other facet of our liaison. I reach out my hand to you and say, let's go before the dreadful feeling of regret within us has a chance to grow, and tell each other that old, incomplete story. I can feel you smiling, or almost smiling, in response to these words of mine. It makes me uncomfortable to picture that smile, it brings to mind sex in changing rooms at the beach, weird hotels, lute menders, runaway train whistles. I'm uncomfortable. Still I hold that we can go on a trip of drunkenness, I say to myself that despite everything, you and I must come together once more; once more with all postponements and preparations considered. I think then of a song of departure for our love affair. Amalia Rodrigues sings a song of primordial melancholy. Moonlight on the beach and the waves, in our hands the cognac glasses left from heaven-knows-what uncompleted, arrested story . . . we lie on our backs and gaze up at the stars. We can relive a very old yearning on one of these stars, I say. We've been there, in that story, for centuries, you reply. I take another sip of my drink. I don't know whether it's the alcohol coursing through my veins and inexorably numbing my body that causes the fantasy to engulf me, or the fact that I can once more consider this aged story with you. Either way the waves, I think, were just as impressive in that story, in those old novels, as they are here. Consequently I feel we can prepare for a long, extremely long night, and as such, I say, must not miss sunrise, at least not this time, we must greet the sun even if with bittersweet joy. You're silent, you suddenly appear to shoot across the sky, just like that star. At that instant our story begins again.

21
Or, the Boundaries of the Manuscript

IN THAT CASE, COULD he explain to Eşref Bey, whom he knew from one of those old stories, that he would like to visit him to discuss these matters, without letting his author know, and talk at necessary length, during the preparation of a manuscript that as yet had no clear destination, of the rationale that might justify his attitude to those who believe in the sacrosanctity of certain old memories? Perhaps at this stage it could all be explained away by pushing the boundaries of a forsaken adventure or a handful of phrases. He must naturally face the consequences of abruptly and once more inviting Eşref Bey to a completely new life. In other words, he must proceed in this new story with the awareness that he'd be judged by those who remembered the events of the past, and the unexpected mistrust that was bound to be awakened in certain minds concerning their author/narrator relationship. Yet he also knew, after all the bodies of text and stylistic experimentation, that he could push certain opportunities as much as he liked, that he could bear down on certain relationships without much thought for the outcomes, and, ultimately, that no relationship in these current days could be set in a solid foundation or be as secure as it outwardly appeared. To boot, nearly everyone was prisoner in one way or another to a certain human habitat, a quandary that incessantly begged to be explained. Since the very first words that he'd attempted to take out of this long script and begin living as his own, he kept finding himself in a story that gave no clues as to where or how it would end. He had no choice now but to monitor this enchantment, this peculiar adventure: a woman with long red hair, blue eyes, and full lips applies makeup in front of a mirror, preparing for an evening that will never be deciphered. Everything seems to be in a haze, as though viewed from behind a curtain of mist. It must be a magical call, from an ancient, timeworn story. The stories will never end but continue on in utterly different manuscripts or people and allude, oftentimes, to utterly different things.

22
My Impromptu Insomnia

IN THAT MANUSCRIPT, YOU had said to me that I could live with a memory, the memory of a lover, or that I could choose to. These were times that I was sick of myself and, I won't lie, rather embarrassed of myself; that I thought I'd undertake certain preparations for the premise of a mere song, that I had a hard time getting my hands on some grass, that I stopped by the whorehouses every weekend, often and easily fell in love, looked in women for a sort of affection that I still have a hard time defining, interrupted my sleep suddenly in the name of what a lover could offer; that I got up in the middle of the night to sit in the most suitable, destitute room in one of the stories, doing nothing, waiting for something undefinable, never tiring of waiting. Yet I had only wished to experience your every breath and call, inhabit you, merely inhabit you; wished to bring to our dreams and our unvoiced isolation the residue of a tattered old journal left over from different people entirely. For me this meant the evocations of a red carnation, the disjointed images of an outdoors movie screening in the summer, the vocalizing of a resistance that would be heard and felt by no one. I had wanted to spread my arms and run, run, run, endlessly run to you. These were words jotted down on the back of an ancient photograph. Could you remember, would you be willing to bear once more, on your terms, the life in that photograph?

23
Eşref Bey Prepares for a Text

IN THESE CIRCUMSTANCES, AT *any point on the avenues of Ergenekon or Kurtuluş or Pangaltı, spying on Eşref Bey by suddenly becoming invisible could be considered a part of the game. It was a world that in many an antecedent manuscript, for the sake of narrating a lengthy and quiet history, his author had obstinately dwelled on and hadn't been able to stop scrutinizing and questioning despite all his efforts. It was merely a premonition that had brought the narrator to this land, borne in these sentences, a premonition which, being inexplicable like all premonitions, gained through this inexplicability another meaning, another value or, as it were, another kind of impunity. He also wished to talk about the desire to rediscover Eşref Bey here in this preparation for a manuscript, despite all the years and stories that had passed, in this land, or recreate and relive him after his own fashion. For this, however, all the old stories must be relived, any wishes to the contrary aside, and transferred to this manuscript despite all obstacles and hesitations. The display windows of the offal shops and fish vendors were once more ablaze with lights tonight, for example, and the way back home susceptible to much gloominess and association. Many stories, written or unwritten, could be remembered, these words providing the path to set out on a different incarnation of an oft-recounted journey. Yet to relive such an acrid past, not from a sense of longing but on behalf of scrutinizing certain losses and resentments, accompanied by a time where each detail was lost a little more with each passing day, that was more his author's concern than his own. Here must also be an outdoor cinema, its screen dappled with thousands, or hundreds of thousands of frames from Turkish movies about tiny unions and lives, a tailor, part confidant, part gossip, and part exile of the night,*

who strove to sew imaginary relationships out of the style pages of
yellowed fashion magazines and filled the fabric with countless
memories to provide warmth, a hat renter who believed he may be
able to relive the old balls once more one day, a superintendent who
mended clocks, a collector of vinyl singles, an epileptic beggar, and,
most importantly, hordes of people who no longer resided here, who
were no longer accommodated, who had been exiled, so to speak, or
without announcement simply passed from this world during this
silent storm. But there was nothing to be done about it now, one
must face the consequences of such an evening no matter what the
circumstances, make do with what was left. In other words, the
unchanging and fundamental matters and melancholies were still
valid, or had to be. At this point, for instance, with the foreboding
of preparing for such an evening, he could make mention of tiny,
bittersweet joys one more time, since Eşref Bey, whom we knew from
that old story or thought we knew, was deeply familiar with both
the deception and the enchantment of these preparations. All said
and done, however, the disappointment of having chosen to live only
in his world, in his own fortress, had come to be a defining factor
in nearly every relationship. For he'd lost all of his friends from that
story; all those who might want to listen to him however briefly or,
for instance, could have felt a song, the evocations of the smell of a
certain kind of pastry or the sorrow over the death of a film star who
had once been the subject of extensive fantasies. Eşref Bey was more
dejected and hopeless in this manuscript than he'd been in that story,
to put it another way. Despite everything, however, there was still
the experience gained from being a character, the little games and
silent escapades he'd discovered thanks to his hope to slyly relate to
his author said experience when the time came for the groundwork
for another character he could one day love with all his being, could
give his all, as well as the strength he derived from another anticipation he could not name. He would attempt, for instance, to stand
in front of the shops whose owners and appearances were long
changed, their display windows that no longer meant anything to
him, not entirely unaware of the possibility of being recognized by

*a long-lost reader or by another character who had in some way or
another contributed to the conception of the story, watching for his
reflection in the glass, with the help of the plays of light he'd mastered, trying to catch his specter that he could never unite with, or
be allowed to unite with, in order to lose himself in the crowd of old
memories; through these images he would try to reach his inner
shadows, to call for them. He went out into these streets almost every
afternoon in the name of this pursuit. It was perhaps the only reason
he never neglected his regular walks. He couldn't have otherwise
endured the thought that despite his best intentions he could no
longer love a city that increasingly alienated him—considering the
hopes he was fast losing as a fictional character who elicited fewer
and fewer opinions—a city where he could no longer drink as much
wine as he wished, the waters of the Bosphorus, tripe soup, and
conversing with newspaper vendors in the small hours of the morning against all kinds of foul weather; his displeasure at never having
been introduced to Monsieur Moiz, who clearly knew these parts
very well, not in a single sentence, and the possibility that his
author's battle with words could go awry at any unanticipated
moment. To top it off, his was no life to be coveted or emulated in
these twilight years he was practically condemned to bear. Now, in
this manuscript, he must hide in Kurtuluş in the bygone room of a
bygone flat of a bygone apartment; he must endure, whether he liked
it or not, his obligatory climb every afternoon to the fourth floor of
this apartment building, in which the lack of an elevator was no
incongruity, ignoring his hemorrhoid, about which he had told no
one, and the griping of his landlady, whose greatest problem in life
was the frequent malfunctioning of the plumbing. And yet the solutions Eşref Bey had found a long, long time ago, when he was still
a main character, might still prove useful for this story as well. In
other words, the option to suspend any conversation could be quite
a relief for everyone who had, one way or another, become tangled
up in the story. Every thought, sentiment, and, most significant of
all, dilemma had the capacity to produce its own feasibility at unexpected moments, after all, and not every situation is as simple as it*

seemed, at least not at this stage. What was the meaning of silence, for instance, for this infinitesimal journey undertaken by the Narrator, who didn't hesitate to endure adverse unions for the sake of scrutinizing his motions? What version of Eşref Bey was the one meant to be kept alive in this manuscript, what sequence of elocutions and images, since certain events were developed, or attempted to be developed, without knowledge of the author? A reader who knew closely the process of writing, the backstage of the previous adventure, who thus believed that certain truths had been warped beyond comprehension while others were cut off quite unexpectedly and downright inappropriately, who wished to enunciate somehow his dissatisfaction and increasing resentment with such a situation, who knew very well how to collaborate with the secret powers in the manuscript and who had important relations at significant points or between nebulous parentheses that not everyone could easily pinpoint, a silent witness who had become unequivocally skilled at presenting certain questions to which there were no answers? Eşref Bey himself, who, being a former teacher of the author, could never get over his instinct to teach and jumped at nearly every halfway-appropriate opportunity to express his disappointment in that lengthy story? Or was the author the undisputable and omnipotent ruler, as is often pointed out, in spite of all these strange games? Was it all thus a singular expression of a game, a deception, of being at a loss for what to do, or of one's inescapable fading? Such questions couldn't be avoided, on this minor, quiet journey, as in the various manuscripts before, and they'd persist in this new dissertation of solitude as long as the irresistible magic of doubt and ambiguity existed. All said and done, however, the Narrator was fighting, for the first time in this manuscript, the battle of directly questioning and indeed by degrees searching for himself. For the first time in many years, as though in a sweet dream or fantasy, everything was under his command again. It was due to this that Eşref Bey's abrupt transposition into this manuscript could be, perhaps, the most plausible part of all this. Of course, that plausibility could well be troubled by the thought that doubt and silence would perpetually reside in us in the name of an infinitely renewable pursuit. Due to his experience, the Narrator seemed to realize the risk. And yet it should still not be overlooked that the same doubts and silences could be tantamount to a minute demonstration of revolt, as Eşref Bey had once witnessed. The bitterness of not saying anything or not being able to say anything in the face of so much wrong. The yearning to create a completely different world, an imaginary island, out of silence and Eşref Bey, or images, smells, and his own inner voice. Thus it would seem that there were many reasons to undertake this forced departure in spite of all contradictions, lack of answers, and the failing of words. After all, one most similar to ourselves could be lurking in a sentence, a word, or a possibility.

24
Images, Fear, and Imaginary Parenthetical Stories

YOU MAY ASSUME NOW that I'm taking a breather, albeit brief, in between a pair of parentheses unknown to anyone, that couldn't possibly be known, that I created just for myself. It's perhaps the rather unsurprising expression of shape-shifting in fragments of text, living like a fugitive among the many sentences I like and dislike and fear visiting, finding myself left over from a handful of bitter joys and wasting away in my fantasy; just another way of starting over a story, a game that will never end, years later with the same words and disappointment and sustaining a lie despite all its harm. There is for instance now a departure I experience on certain nights, carried along the breeze of lost joys, hangouts, or the voices of people that turn into a long, lingering song. I listen to some music at such times, have a little to drink, and come close to fearing myself and the residue of these words within me; I want to talk and talk and talk to someone about my nearly non-negotiable resolution to journey along this well-known solitude. I know this is an ancient, ancient resentment, a shame, even. To tell the truth, however, there's no longer any significance to be found in bearing this shame in nearly every relationship or possible discourse or to seem accepting of my defeat after every story, clandestine departure, or night voyage. I yearn to finally tell my author this, to lay it bare at the most appropriate point of this new adventure. I find it meaningless and unnecessary, for instance, to be introduced as a man who speaks only of himself in front of a lover, expecting something of his past and experiences, after all the debacles no less; I live in fear of being painted once more as a protagonist who would attempt to impress a prospective lover with a favored poem or song. At such times I prefer to take a breather within a pair of parentheses, doing my best to forget about lost battles, tiny revolts, crowded Saturday nights, and certain emotional topographies; I attempt once more to make do with mere dreams on this diminutive and rather privileged island that my author, despite all his efforts, can't lay his hands on. All that's left behind then is the call of a few seagulls and the vision of migrating birds and imaginary cities only told of in books, and I say to myself: images, images, images. It's an ancient, ancient song, reminding me of you, your unresponsiveness and your refusal to come here. It's then that I think I could give that familiar smile another go, saying to myself that many a hallucination or nightmare could fittingly accompany this hopeless anticipation. I picture then the people on their fresh pursuits in brand-new stories, recalling the unrestrained and unrestrainable assault of words, the stars, the September evenings, and the prolonged breakfasts. I become uncomfortable. There are things I can't express, I say to myself. I give up.

25
Faces, the Streets, Hopeless Shadow Theaters

NO MATTER THE PATHS *leading to him, it would have been inevitable for the Narrator to find Eşref Bey at a time he held onto his daydreams of his lover, struggling with all his strength not to lose them. As such, it was maybe necessary to resume this little journey after a meeting liable to take place at such a moment. The meeting was initially uncomfortable for Eşref Bey. After all those years, evasions, and attempts at erasing his tracks and hiding between parentheses, it was neither easily comprehensible nor tolerable to be forced to remember those old faces and to relive all the resentments, uncertainties, and half-finished notes. Yet the Narrator knew by heart the magic words that would allow him to move between manuscripts and enter into deep and exceptional relations with certain characters. From here on, for instance, he would try another dimension of time with Eşref Bey, during which he would tell him that they followed the lead of an entirely different story from that old one; he would also tell his author, in the name of creating a conciliatory phrase, no matter how trivial, that he was quite aware of the notes he had taken once upon a time and that certain behaviors and his journey amongst the line breaks were explicable through these very notes, which was the sole reason he wouldn't betray their implications; with some level of conscientiousness he would speak of unanswered and unanswerable questions, heartbreak, and the feeling of being exiled from a person. All else aside, he had a measure of responsibility for his author not being able to sufficiently explain his impulse to depart on a journey where it had been clear from the beginning he'd be out of his depth, and it behooved him, whether he wished to or not, to present an explanation, an offering of peace. To top it off, he had possibly hoisted upon his author, with this appeal and the experimentations in style in this bizarre, arbitrarily progressing love story, the risk of being one who loitered and seemed in the eyes of some to often repeat himself. Of course, it was entirely possible to approach the problem from a different angle. Any expla- nation he made regarding the matter, however, in other words any truths he exposed, may cause him to be rejected from subsequent manuscripts, effectively sentencing him to complete obsolescence, by this person whose instability should be accepted by mere virtue of his being an author. Being a willing exile was one thing; being an unwilling exile, on the other hand, another thing entirely. Certainly there was a place, indefinable and tasting of resentment, where the two overlapped, in which sense, obligation, and willingness could merge and compensate one another. Yet whatever yearnings one harbored, would one not hope to count on the prospect of a place, a warm breath, that one could eventually return to and seek sanctuary in? That was the reason that being thrown out of and completely exiled from a lengthy body of text was so abhorrent, making it impossible to endure for the sake of an identity embraced without much thought. It shouldn't have been so difficult after so many stories to try on various masks and roles, but despite the jealousy, plagiarism, and Byzantine scheming in the literary world there was no question of him being accepted, in his present state, into another manuscript by another author. As it was, such a union could make sense with a clandestine offering of mediation. The effect of certain old memories, this realm of memories often misconstrued as yearn- ing for a traditional, well-worn past and just as often misused for a number of personal ends, on the author was a roundly well- acknowledged fact, after all. Further insult shouldn't be added to injury by extensively criticizing the attempt to take advantage of an image, the call of an age-old story. Confronted with these words and believing himself to be the subject of an unexpected joke, if not a rather frustrating game, Eşref Bey imagined the Narrator to be the author himself appearing before him in disguise, and abruptly blurted out something in Sephardic. He was relieved to notice that his little attempt had thrown the Narrator, realizing he had no reason to be alarmed. For the author's reaction to this odd phrase and its singular evocations would have been wholly dissimilar, such an attitude abruptly steering the conversation to the truth of life and literature and the obligation to choose; mutual balances of power once more gauged and, for that matter, groundwork laid for a variety of resentments. But the current situation was different, no doubt about it. It appeared that Eşref Bey was confronted with a simple, highly suggestible, and shape-shifting Narrator and a fictional character that had borne here many characteristics from an array of acquaintances. Was this a kind of injustice, did this approach once again make him victim to his testiness and firm adherence to principle? All else aside, what kind of stalemate had brought him here to this unexpected meeting, what phrases had acted as carriers of what meanings or evocations? As his author often said, these must be the kinds of questions made beautiful by their absurdity. That was partly the reason he approached the Narrator with equal measures of affection and pity. "We don't have much time, wherever we happen to live or exist, we're all in our way counting the minutes," he said, adding simply, in spite of all the sentiments he wished to relay and share, "not to mention, as a fictional character with both writing and acting chops, I feel you shouldn't bore your readers with our protracted dialogues any longer." Despite the importance of the visit, he didn't offer the Narrator anything to drink. After all, unless there was an external or artificial intrusion, fictional characters couldn't give or offer anything, other than words, to one another. To put it the orthodox way, that was one of the most important rules of the game. "I'm listening," he said and, full of hope once more for a brand-new story despite all the words and time that had passed, added with vigor, "let's hear what kind of love this is and, for that matter, if need be, let's see if we can live together, even if only for the duration of this text."*

26
The Wind that Wraps around the Manuscript

I SET SAIL NOW for the vision of a cove where the sea and the forest embrace. I say to myself, this is an island I carried inside me from heaven-knows-where, a coastal town left over from an age-old retreat, almost sensing that the longing tied to this faraway terrain might sooner or later force me to a lengthy manuscript that will be difficult to complete, not to mention live in. To encounter you, on the other hand, in an unanticipated turn of phrase, along the way learning about where, with whom, and in the name of what longings *you* lived, that will once more necessitate recalling certain defeats. I'll then have to satisfy myself by singing to you the song of a breakup I myself never endured. You'll perceive that I can inhabit and feel you surprisingly well despite the distance between us and see that I already know the themes you hadn't had the chance to tell me. An inexpressible shiver will overtake your senses. Perhaps that's why for this manuscript I'm considering a light, penetrating wind; a wind I could never stop living, relating, despite the dozens of hostile stares that it draws. I fall silent, feeling deeper comprehension of those old resentments. I'd like to exit this body of text without saying anything to anyone. Leaving without knowing where I'm going. For nights of such yearning, I muse, a coffee and a glass of cognac should be thought of. Such dilemmas and obsessions don't embarrass me anymore as much as they used to. It reoccurs to me without bidding, however, that I won't be able to share for many years that photograph, and the many details in it, with another person.

27
Action, My Friend, Mere Action

IN AN ADVENTURE, THE Narrator spoke of the opportunities in tracking down a story, told Eşref Bey of his intentions for setting out on this adventure, how as much as he tried, he'd never be able to share this story with another to his heart's desire, his deep fear of the consequences of such a situation, how he felt these days on the brink of disappearing or at an unexpected junction with his author, the reasons for his not knowing whether he could ever go back to the old stories, and most significantly, that all the dreams he'd built on the expectation of prospective love had been razed by this defeat. "The frustration of love," replied Eşref Bey in turn, "is that everyone, almost everyone, will continuously bear a defeat experienced at least once into other relationships, love affairs, and probabilities. No matter what occurred then, the resentment persists, continues to live inside us and prod us here and again. And it seems everyone is fond of being prisoner to the same old lovers and resentments. In your case, however, there was something wrong from the beginning and consequently an unavoidable ending, as our author often puts it, or as it were, a stalemate. Your obligatory experiences, your encounters and endurances, ought to have been warning enough that you would be swept into such a predicament, if you get my meaning. Such modes of appeal regrettably no longer have validity in human relationships, especially not in our passages to a lover. Such sensibility has never won, was never as effective as assumed in cultivating passion. I'm obliged to talk to you once more of superiority, the irresistible lure of arrogance, no matter its nature or form. Action, my friend, mere action. This phrase may remind you of teetering on the brink of crucial decisions. In human relations, however, it doesn't get more real than this, no other adventure or

*way of life that can be achieved through words and nuanced sensi-
bility. No such lover or affair either, for that matter. All the songs,
tales, and poems, in that sense, have always been the expression of
this lie, quest, or defeat." Lies and deception. It wasn't the first time
that the Narrator had been confronted with the idea that he had
made up this love, this longing, in his imagination, and given it
a home there. Yet he seemed to be the only one who couldn't grasp
this truth fully, the only one who wished to accept the lie as the
most fundamental and unchanging condition of living humanely.
Presently he could not talk to Eşref Bey about the hope his lover had
engendered in him despite everything, the inner monologues that
seemed never-ending, the awakenings that preceded nightmares,
the imaginary meal consumed at the Chinese restaurant, and the
ever-shifting array of visions. Since they were here, however, he was
obliged to trust certain evocations or touch upon certain old defeats
once more. "A matter as though of always loving a Raşel," he said in
turn, "but the day comes in a relationship when you're faced with
unexpected answers or developments. What is your response, for
instance, to the fact that years after your unforgettable conversations,
our author donned the guise of another narrator and found Raşel
in Tel Aviv, wrote the story one day despite all objections and never
forgot you despite your protracted estrangement? Does observing all
this not light even the smallest candle of hope in the name of believing in the possibilities of a love for those of us who have no choice but
to constantly experience and accept defeat?" "Accepting defeat . . .
you make it difficult for me," said Eşref Bey, struggling to interpret
after his own fashion the story of which he'd once been the protagonist, "to answer this question, for I would be able to approach you
with two very different attitudes. First, I should say that I lost my
function in the story after a certain point and so cannot be held
accountable for those years of Raşel's that I didn't experience. The
best part of that story, I should point out, was that after a certain
period of our lives, Raşel and I were not brought together. In such
a case love didn't end but carried on its possibilities within you in
spite of all the pain, the people, and the resentments. That may have*

been the best part of the love we experienced and by all accounts would keep experiencing for many long years. After all, it gave you the chance to constantly keep alive and nurture a possibility, allowed you to keep putting off that little death. Now let's get to the second approach. In this, I can attempt to approach the matter from a different point of view, shedding my limited function in the story as well as all the restrictions of time and place imposed upon me. That would mean acquiescing to the game you've proposed. As such, years later I can endeavor certain interpretations and claim, for the sake of making a reprimand, however infinitesimal, that so many of my most important aspects and traits were neglected and disregarded by my author. It isn't really possible, sadly, to deny the idea that each person exists in others in different forms and incarnations. Ultimately, however, no matter the experiences or possibilities, our author is likely to be perceptive about this pain, this inescapable impasse. Should you appeal to him, however, to put together the story and make it available for the desired people to see, using to your advantage, if a little selfishly, that feeling of obligatory solidarity, he's likely in turn to endeavor a new inner battle concerning what problems to tackle or avoid tackling and as a result take the completely different tack of approaching things as though their implications and consequences held little weight, undertaking an attempt at a discourse that will seem interesting to some and alienating to many. That will be the understandable, justifiable expression of self-defense and self-preservation that he hopes will be viewed as unconscious. None of these methods are acceptable to me, someone who knows him closely, any longer. All else aside, I have very, very serious doubts that the story will be able to reach its true protagonists, who are very far away from it nowadays. Isolation is a difficult thing to relate, as you know."

28
Appearing As Though Living

IT SEEMED IN THAT manuscript as though we would once more undertake small hopes and concealments, endeavoring once more to play around with our fears of death. It would be through you that this text would be written, in other words, and we'd meet in a sentence in a distant story. In this manuscript we would remember everything we had forgotten, bearing the uneasiness of moving toward one another, if only in a dream. Fast beside me were suggestions, nebulous words, sentences that never seemed to come to an end, and talk, talk, talk. Stories expressing heartbreak always begin with such an awakening, with the residue of a nightmare, an intoxication, and sorrow, I said to myself then. I smiled. I had no reason to believe in the truth of that statement. All else aside, it isn't my job to write but only to live out those stories, or appear as though I were living them out, I also remarked at that instant. Appearing as though living, yes. This would be an understandable extension of the complicity I had entered into with those who wished to share the story with me. Maybe at that moment I had envisaged the sting of being washed up from a nightmare, one in which I moved toward you with all my uneasiness. It was all as it was before, naturally, as we had left it the previous evening. I knew that a magic touch could change the appearance of this tiny room. After all, everything was now possible or seemed so in the literary world, with all its attempts and undertakings. Yet an imprisonment, my imprisonment by you, my dreams, and thus also myself, must also be underscored to the utmost. With my years of experience I was capable of understanding at least this much, of evaluating at least this much of the matter. I well could run the risk of progressing toward this brief manuscript, in spite of all my uneasiness, for the sake of just a little joy. Following this phase, I obeyed the rules of the game and sensed that it all went on as before. It was morning to boot, and in my bed I seemed to become more silent, lonely, and secretive with each passing day. I asked myself how long this sense of being lost would last, and how many more words, deceptive consolations, and tales it would sweep me into before it ended. I was imbued then with details, the lives, loves, and most of all the lovelessness that many hoped to build with the poetry and irresistible allure of details. I recalled the rooms, isolations, and untaken voyages, once more coming closer to understanding that you and I would never live out that story as I wished we could. Living out a story. This must have been one of the dreams or phrases one returned to again and again. It seemed to contain a song I'd been trying for years to describe, a song that unexpectedly evoked a fresh new morning and the Aegean sun. The Aegean sun indeed, you, your distance, and all the things I can't tell you were the Aegean sun. Namely, did certain mornings dawn on an Aegean island upon small joys, possibilities, and singular eroticisms? What sun had woken you in the tiny room of a bed-and-breakfast run by an old Rum[2], whose ties were still intact despite the years and the forced exile, on an Aegean island, what small joys swelled within you? Did you try sailing out to the blueness, into the peerless scent of the sea, leaving it all, all, all behind? Did the fragrance of the sea settle into your hair in those days? Did you wander through the marketplace of that island that I can now only daydream about? And did you share the evenings of such days with your lover at one of the restaurants on the beach, drawing your bare feet through the sand as you enjoyed something to drink, some joy, and *mezedes*? Associations, associations, associations. Associations, yes, and the various ways we fail to unite. That's perhaps the reason why I can't shake off the idea of recalling once more the extension of that nightmare, within me

---

2   *Rum* are Turkish citizens of Greek origin

and the manuscript alike, or of reliving them in words, albeit in a completely different dimension: I was riding out of Istanbul in a strange car that I was unable to drive at a slower pace. It seemed to be the kind of car left over from an unusual dream or an unwritten story, whose shape and appearance in my memory shifted constantly, expecting reckless acts from me that I could not and would never carry out. I can't explain to myself, despite myself, where this road is taking me and, more importantly, I see no detail around me that could qualify as a clue. I was simply on a lengthy, almost unending road heading to an unknown, indefinable destination; despite all my preparations, words, and hoarded possibilities, that seemed to be all. Perhaps you had said that you'd only stay in this manuscript briefly, that your preparations were for other people entirely and lives you couldn't describe. I had managed, finally, to stop dwelling on everything, on my stories to which the vision of you lent meaning, for night upon night upon night, to leave behind my tiny stories, tiny connections, and tiny postponements. In that case I ought to be imbued with a sense of enormous joy, I ought to convince myself that the place I'm headed to is one so many people dream of and dedicate stories and poems to. To top it off, I'd be able to free myself from this city that had kept me prisoner for years. Yet after these ruminations the problem seemed to surface once more in a new form. I was constantly dogged by the thought of not knowing where you were inside the manuscript. It was the start of a whole new, dissimilar dead end, a prolonged and habituated scrutiny. Would I for example be able to reach you, be united with you, after such yearning? Or could it be that I had never been invited to this manuscript, not ever, not by anyone, had I created everything from scratch in my dreams, in my isolation or as you once said, in my head? Was I once more on the trail of an aged, undefined hallucination? Questions, fear, and the lack of answers. As always and indeed, despite all my efforts, I couldn't answer these questions. The only thing I was aware and sure of was that I was riding along on this road at a speed that was fast spinning out of my control. Still I persisted with all my might and my delusions in searching for an unexpected clue, a keyword. Right then, at that moment, I came upon a fork in the road. It was a brief, infinitesimal, instant of hesitation, a time without hope of return or expression; it was as though I should continue this manuscript though I inwardly resisted at every turn the risky, lethal possibilities. A plaintive, velvety song approached us at this point in our narrative. A song, yes, barely there, warm, reminiscent of a lullaby; evoking a life far, far away, now lost, gaining meaning with insufficiently constructed recollections of a garden, the sea, and solitude, a song somewhat synonymous with tired breakfasts, the grogginess of untold dreams, and impossible homecomings. In truth it was the miniature earthquake that had made itself felt one way or another in words and never-ending sentences, a storm of remembrance told often and striven to be shared; it possessed the quality of preparing and calling one to the tiny deaths once chanced by others. That may have been why I continued on one of those roads as though I had resolved it all, at least partly why the apparent simplicity of it hadn't seemed odd to me. Siderakis, the church of Aya Nikola, the Rum Primary School. The key sentence must be hidden in these words or their associations. I was almost assured now that the road I traveled would lead me to you. After a while, however, I would run into an obstruction I hadn't anticipated, a sort of roundabout, a road that was increasingly circular. The key sentence seemed to be calling me to that truth, the little death, no matter how much I resisted. It was the story of the same old dream, the same old return. I was permeated at that moment with familiar melancholy, and it was now the joy of a separation I was no stranger to, a departure to an island, that I was experiencing. There were the tales, words, and delusions I was once more bringing along, as well as the song that poured through me incessantly. At that I thought you might be able to comprehend, sooner or later, that I had set out on this voyage for you. I knew very well also this sense of surrender. Also with me were defeats, silences, and old deceptions. We'd bear the island's story to one another along with a whole new array of agony and dreams.

29
An Old, Age-Old Old Dream

"TO BE PERFECTLY HONEST, *it will be somewhat inevitable for those who read this conversation of ours to think of us as downright weak in the presence of the author,*" the Narrator replied, "*yet we both know very well that the matter is not, nor should be, anything like that. For at such times I say to myself that we can vanish from these manuscripts at certain times and reunite, in the name of fresh possibilities with entirely different people, between the lines, imperceptibly in parentheses, or conversations that could have several meanings; we can resist the Author's bullying, his often-erratic bearing, and his experiments in style that are alienating to many as it is, we can ultimately succeed in becoming more trustworthy, more tenable characters; refusing suggestions is, I think, tantamount to knowing how to refuse and agreeing to face the consequences, hoping once more for something I have trouble naming or defining; I want to dream, as much as I can and against all our hopelessness and unforgettable defeats, that a life can be built upon a pursuit, and can never forget that a dream that ends can very well be the same thing as death knocking upon the door. The strength that drew me to this story or engendered such a story within me could be explained away, in that case, by the expression of a certain emptiness. Losses and disenchantments would always be wounding, of course. Yet ultimately one still says he's glad to have tried, that it was worth trying, and is often capable of constructing a dream of the future once more inside his never-ending isolation.*" "*A story of resistance,*" said Eşref Bey, smiling a little, "*it's an old, such an old dream. At certain times many yearnings seem achievable. One day, however, perhaps many years after the action, we may find the unexpected sound of regret chasing us. Have we done a disservice to those who contributed in some way or another to the development of our characters? Do we both not sense, now and then, in this involuntary journey between manuscripts, that the only thing left to the author after all his fancies and attempts will be words, that no matter the commentary and directions in a story the reader will still interpret things their own way, that this is the singular expression of a top-secret complicity? I know, I know, you'll want to speak to me once more of the deceptive and unreliable quality of words, of the certain emotions they fall short of describing, pointing out that as much as you wish, there's no escaping the fact that you'll be face-to-face with your author some way down the manuscript, having to risk a reckoning. We've all once faced, were forced to face, similar reckonings even if the words and methods were different, we all suffered the consequences of the prospective stories after our own fashion. The one important difference was perhaps that you wished to take this confrontation a few steps further and live your own life despite any obstacles. For many, your attitude was tantamount to betrayal. A betrayal committed against the author by his closest, most reliable friend. This too is a very, very old story, but I fear everyone that contributed to the conception of the text will have to face the consequences. Word gets around, as you can see, and it's arrived at discussion over the structure of the text or its creation process, which has had many preoccupied for some time. To achieve more, at least considering the conditions and style of the text, would have been downright undoable, unthinkable. It all depends from this point on on the results of the suspension of our rights to freedom, and their secession to our author, through his own means, for the sake of the manuscript's health and endurance. It's a dangerous game we can't stop playing despite our awareness of its risks, a game that slaps us in the face with the loathsomeness of conformity. In such situations, the most we're willing to comment is that our small hopes and spaces of freedom, as dubiously reliable as they are, should live on in all of us in the name of a murky future. At this stage the only thing I might miss is sharing the handful of sentiments lent meaning by the strength I've derived from our secret pact, I may, with some timidity, ask a small favor of you. If you like, you may see it as a part of the small rebellion you've long dreamed of: please don't tell our author, when your fateful encounter occurs, that you've seen me in this state. For there's a certain Eşref Bey that he created in his head for better or for worse and welcomed to this story with all his purity of heart and sensibility. An Eşref Bey whose present life he has no knowledge of, who he firmly believes has died. An Eşref Bey who still hasn't stopped resorting to the old resentments and petty games, who still struggles to haul his own rock in his own fashion up his tiny hill without making a show of it but, to tell the truth, a rather overblown, overprized Eşref Bey. Yet how did we get to this point, why couldn't we content ourselves with the old stories, what people, misconceptions, and deceptions did we fall victim to? Why were we so feeble dealing with words? I don't know, sadly, I just don't know. I can no longer answer to my heart's desire these questions, to me once worth positing in every form, easily ignoring the doubts and tremors within me. Can we meet again years later, talk once more of the magic and unease of reckoning, or will a word, a pair of parentheses, or an unexpected punctuation mark drive us even further away from here—that I can't say, either. Whatever the possibilities, in the name of the intertextual solidarity of characters you hold to such esteem, please accept my appeal and my muteness. The intertextual solidarity of characters indeed. I feel it safe to assume that this proposal will draw an unexpected noise from unexpected places, paragraphs, or the tenuous spaces between the lines."*

30
If You Only Knew

PRESENTLY I FEEL AS though I'm returning to a manuscript, the narrative of an age-old turn of phrase. It appears to be a phrase left unfinished in the face of a multitude of people, relationships, and desires that couldn't be fulfilled, and was imbued with meaning through the associations of new words entirely, a phrase that might in time lengthen, transform, and be borne away to a whole new manuscript, even, who knows, to a whole new discourse. There are things I adamantly continue to do here despite all my hopelessness, to put it another way. On such days I think of all the things I couldn't grow inside my heart with you. In truth it's all the details and lives I accumulated to this day that perhaps never held as much significance as one might hope, from people and lovers whom I'd thought I knew and put on a pedestal for the empty hope of a dream. We never read Edip Cansever or Turgut Uyar or Zingo Kosovich together, for instance, never listened to Mahler, Amalia Rodrigues, Hümeyra, Mahmuri, Efendi, or Andon Mexis, never visited the quaint coffeehouse by the sea that I depicted with different passions and desires in mind entirely, never had fried mussels there; never shared a film with stolen kisses and naps, never plotted to murder someone, never experienced the giddiness of stealing a book from a library, never got plastered and sang stupid songs in the streets, never slapped one another, never threw water in one another's face, never got lost in the deeply silent street of an unfamiliar city in the darkest hour of night, never stuck gum on cab windows, no matter where, never had our picture taken in a photo booth, never extended a night of coffee, cognac, cigarettes, and sex into the first light of day, never wandered wantonly along

93

an endless beach on a summer evening, never bought each other
gifts, however modest, with a possible parting of ways in mind,
I never told you I wanted to have a child with you, never had
you clean my pipes and shine my shoes, my glasses, and my
writing desk, never taught you to curse in Spanish, never had
you give me a Thai massage, never suggested that you shower in
my bathroom nor that you do a headstand and sing. As you see,
my darling, despite it all, our disappointments, disaffections, and
forced exiles, we could still have found many details or attempts
at joy to proliferate at will. These were dreams that could bind
to the earth someone like me who has no choice but to live. You
could maybe have given meaning to my life by acceding to the
role of lover, if for a short while. Ultimately your voyage was on
a different island entirely, one far, far away from me. Your departure seemed as though it were to a whole other lover, a zest for
life I could never fully trust in. In that case we could have forced
open the door to new choices with such words as: all that's left
behind are memories, and after all, everyone is the passenger of
their own path, their own pursuit, and their own solitude. All
aside, many words to this day have become many different words
in various manuscripts and attempts at phrasing. Yet if you only
knew how frightening and wounding it is to be the one left
behind at the station, for all that once again, once again, once
again, now, after all this time and more importantly, all these
attempts. If you only knew how badly I want to describe to you
the wound and the desperation. Yet the days and the nights that
always beg to be described differently though they're constantly,
constantly repeated, as well as the seasons that rotate in the same
painful way, keep annihilating or at the very least shaking up
something in our lives. At such times we may say, for instance,
that we're being summoned by a brand-new voice, an ancient
song budding within us. It's reminiscent of the call of old days,
old clothes, forgone journeys, uneaten meals, and the night.
All the conditions are set now in order to remember the words
that will remain behind: I came then upon a twist in the road,

a punctuation mark I was no stranger to, I wished for a watch I may have left behind in a sentence to steal away an eons-old solitude. I expected something from you, you see, something that far surpassed memories and words. Yet now I'm only left with unease, insecurity, and deeply private regrets within. I'm here in this sentence, the sentence to which you never came and never will. Silence and melancholy pour through me once again and I turn into a word, a possibility you will never come to be.

31
If That Resentment, That Call, That Isolation Had Never Been

"YOU CAN REST ASSURED *that I'll do the best I can," said the Narrator, with a measure of apprehension. "To tell the truth, I would rather have had this conversation in much different circumstances. In other words, when I was coming here or chancing this encounter, I had hoped for more than the spaces between the lines. Yet whatever dimension of time and space we were living in, there was no assurance that we wouldn't encounter this impediment to expression again. Postponements. You'll comprehend much more, I think, if I merely utter the word 'postponements,'" he said, attempting to express his understandable chagrin over the matter. From this point on, however, Eşref Bey didn't speak again. His silence must mean, at least for this long manuscript, that the conversation was once again no sooner started than finished. At this, the Narrator exited without a word this cell of isolation or engrossment. His steps were synonymous with a certain unpreventable return to a prosaic story, but there wasn't much to be done about it. As he descended the stairs of the hoary apartment, the sound of an elderly woman singing, with a hint of a Rum accent and accompanied by the piano, the song of Ramona with an affect like Mistinguett's. "Could it be?" he murmured to himself in eagerness. He changed his mind, however, choosing with some deliberation and a measure of obligation to ignore the call of his inner voice, or more accurately, his intuition. He couldn't risk going any further after this stage, these conversations, and most significantly, this story. When he went out onto the street he noticed that it had gotten quite late and night had fallen. The moon had risen with all its enchantment, allure, and perplexity. The moon and its associations, he said to himself then,*

96

thinking of how the moon was genderless in this realm of language to which he owed everything, as opposed to those others he occasionally dabbled in. It may have been beautiful to think of the moon as a female, a woman who was suggestive of death. This wasn't the time, however, to dwell on any of this. Darkness had crept into the streets and very interiors of the houses, causing everyone who lived by day and so-called daylight to withdraw into his own silence or sanctuary. The price of civilization (!) would be extracted more harshly with each passing day. He'd experienced this feeling before, as well as the history of these apartments and the pangs of these little deaths, or at least had appeared to. A cool breeze now blew through these streets. He was no stranger to either the sentence or the associations that could be linked to it. Everything else aside, it was just the right weather for the end of a story. All that one could do now was to bask in the lover, the enchantment cast by the lover. For this, regrettably, one had only words, words, words. Words, yes, that which could never be reliable in the full sense, which could not be brought to life in another. In this story, as in all the other stories, no question had found satisfying answers, no detail had been relished enough to leave no room for doubt, no disappointment described in full color. In the end, however, the call was always there, the need for it would always reside within us. Could we otherwise explain our resistance to these defeats or our departures to a whole new story on certain nights of solitude?

32
A Hell Springs Then to My Mind

THAT'S PARTLY THE REASON I now rejoice in my being able once more to get lost in the crowd of words. It's a bitter kind of joy that I'm no stranger to, the price of which I paid years, many years ago, in accordance with the rules of the game. A glimpse of eternity where the act of writing, no matter for what or for whom, gains meaning, no matter how slight, and becomes redeemable. A hell springs then to mind and I struggle again to shake free of magic words, deadly voyages, goddesses of regret, and the fear of witnessing my own burial. Others, others, others, I say to myself then, we know this phrase, you know this phrase, we played that game for better or for worse, you played that game. But there's no going back now, no going back, that dream is gone, the phrase gone, the opposite shore gone. At this point, not being able to make out the end of the road, knowing you can keep moving, keep moving in that realm despite it all, ought to be this adventure's one and only assurance.

33
Separations or What Hides in Hidayet's Painting

"AFTER ALL THE PEOPLE *unmentioned, all the refuges unsought, all the hands, fancies, and ways of muteness, I now seem to find, in this book, something that suddenly walks and advances toward me," thought Hidayet, feeling troubled in a way he believed he couldn't define or share with the quite unrelenting progression of words. Rather uneasy, he looked out of the window of his house into the street he'd spent the bulk of his life in, not wishing to remember the remnants of worn-out hopes, the trees, the balances built, and the chimney cleaners. Old and decrepit houses that continued to exist by externalizing a kind of sulkiness rose to his mind unbidden, as well as intoxications, cul-de-sacs, the deceptiveness of safe days and relationships, and Maurice Utrillo, making him understandably and tolerably anxious at the frequency of their influx in so brief an instant; he perceived that for years he had made do with watching, merely watching this street and the people to whom it gave meaning through his window. He then questioned when and where it might have been that the error first began, wanting to scrutinize despite its risks the disconsolation of remaining a spectator, of not being able to get lost in a picture for all his hopes. Could resigning himself to one of the minor, more obscure roles in this play be explained by the inability to risk great defeats or losses, for example, or by fleeing from himself to spite himself? Yet what exactly was it, the peculiar tale of the enchanted role in this protracted play, that allowed for experiencing all sorts of stages in all their forms, by what standards could it be defined? What could you change and how, so to speak, by attempting to persist on stage, could you through this persistent lingering prove success of some sort, or some small victory? Could you express to your heart's desire your timeworn struggle? In order to* remain in the game, did everyone not abide by some form or another of compensation, muteness, increasingly a compromise, and by extension now and then a member of the audience? Did everyone not experience somewhat the delusion of the places and lives they couldn't reach? Did the victories not, by and large, lead many to the same conundrum, to becoming another's hell, victim, or executioner? These were the kinds of questions that had never and could never really be asked. That was partly the reason that Hidayet thought, "We can still return to the starting point if we're willing to take the risk of a whole new set of associations," shuddering with the elation of receiving a call from this thoroughly and glaringly incomplete book on this spring morning. On the spring evenings that he watched the street from his window, he would often think of how little he'd reveled in certain delights, inciting in him the wish to share his resentments, his jealousies that hid behind an irrepressible form of self-defense, with at the very least a picture, or the adventure of a picture. In his life in reality, however, were only pictures, forbidden, designed, borne in hopes and disenchantments; those days also tasted slightly of a preparation for a bittersweet kind of joy, for hope and for another. His consciousness would then be impelled by imprecise images from years ago when he'd been lauded as an efficacious art teacher, he'd hear once more the monotony, a monotony he knew well from previous stories, of the hours he spent in the small partition of the living room, where he studied the often rather tiresome drawings of his students, he'd then resentfully find himself heading toward the sounds of the evening's dinner preparations, pondering evasions, obligatory silences, and unrealized longings. Nothing had changed since then or, to be more accurate, a kind of timelessness or another concept of time entirely ought to be devised for such a story. "An art teacher who has lost the picture of his dreams," he murmured to himself then, in some manner deriving a measure of hope from the words. The details conceived up to this point may very well suffice for the expression of monotony or a stalemate. Now, the leftovers of a quotidian familial order could be added on top of all this. For the sake of this order, for instance, the *names of children, who were still growing and would in time strive to go their own ways, could be recollected. A girl and a boy, as Necatigil said in that renowned poem of his, a girl and a boy for everyone so we may say that all is in order. Obligatory visits, trivial holiday plans, everyday political developments, and the unresolved murders of truths, truths postponed, sensed somewhere within but left unexpressed, were also part of this order or among the probabilities of this choice. All was in order, yes, in such fugitive instants all was in order. But what about what could never be shared in these instants, what of the sounds or the pictures that were never drawn and could never be? In the living room, the aged corner that he'd embraced as a tiny space of freedom, Hidayet at that moment was forced once more to look at one of the paintings he'd somehow had the courage to meticulously frame and hang on the wall, suffused with bittersweet gladness at remembering that there was someone other than himself who knew its secret, its real secret; a gladness that was reminiscent of the one he'd experienced at the moment he had sensed that this story that he believed incomplete could be resumed in another, entirely different, and special voice. No one other than us knows where the hidden face in the schoolyard is, that which lends this painting its real heart, he said to himself. It was in reality a customary, familiar voice that now and then returned to this fugitive life, encasing within its own longing, in other words the echo of a call, a resentful call, embodied in this tiny, bygone painting: it was as though I had coincidentally crossed paths with you like in the age-old song, and in our early days you, with your gaze, your face that to me still seems impossible to define and depict in paint, and your inaccessible loneliness were like the harbinger of an imprisonment that could stretch out over many years. What had I seen in you back then, how had we progressed toward one another, what dilemmas and dangers endeavored along the way? What debacle could your mandatory transfer from another school to the one I was teaching in cause to recur? Why did you stay at that school so briefly? Because you believed that I, that we, couldn't handle the consequences of a passion that allowed us to say everything to the other with a mere look, our impossibility, because you knew that we could resume certain paintings even if we became estranged, or perceived that either way you would eventually transition into the adventure that you sensed you couldn't share with anyone but me? Was this going through your mind when you smiled at me, for the first time and last time and with great sorrow and hopelessness, as I toiled at painting the schoolyard at those hours of an evening, was that why you left this school after a very, very brief time here, for the sake of other passions and silences? Why did you have to appear and disappear from my life in an instant, to put it another way? Why, as with many of my prior relationships, did I end up having to ask myself whether or not this extremely short-lived relationship had been only a dream? Had I found something in your gaze that I had lost somewhere along the way, had the lines of your face been the declaration of the unrealized longings of my past? Why was our passion synonymous with our separation, with a regret, or with shame? Why didn't I pursue you, why did we set out in search of new pictures? Why does the hum of people talking in this school that I'll soon not be coming to any longer, after being seen off with, perhaps, a modest gathering, sound to me like the song of everlasting captivity? By what measurements and code of ethics could we explain our natural, so-called regular sexuality, why these ruthless truths, in spite of all the pain and disappointment, the tiny paradises that were or could yet be lost? Did they, the ones we could not stop living among, of whom we were a part, our prejudices, our inner turmoil, our little deaths, really know the meaning of sexuality, did we, for that matter? Paintings in which sexuality, a very special sort of sexuality, was depicted in a few vague brushstrokes, the manner in which two smudges of paint coalesced. The expression of an expansive passion, as almost always a dead end, a forced retreat. Where was the lover now, how old was she? Why were such relationships always synonymous with such losses, why did those who didn't shy away from breaking up come together in impossibility no matter their experience? Why did they always run toward a nightmare, why the difficulty in uninhibitedly relaying and more importantly, sharing certain pictures and stories? Would it not change and enrich, if marginally, the history of relationships if the paintings that depicted loss, intensity, escape, and imprisonment as a sanctuary or probable loss were as renowned as those that were shown, that saw the light of day? Hidayet then considered that these questions might one day be turned into a long and bitter manuscript by an art historian wishing to depict this timeworn life, understandably preferring not to bring to mind his deceptions and the ludicrous situations he'd found himself in due to his faith in such viabilities. This story could merge with another and one day become legible, these paintings may perhaps reach the faraway lover yet. This was the adventure of a dangerous passion, the adventure of illicit emotions and of those who knew how to surrender a life to a passion. Yet he himself knew very well that no matter how hard one tried, no matter what longings, resentments, or stories one endured, he really only loves a single lover in his lifetime. The reflections of love and passion resonate within us throughout our own eternity; unsaid sentences are borne into new longings or delusions. Reading this book, Hidayet had experienced a bittersweet joy at the fact that a hopeless passion, untenable in any familiar form or realm, had also been withstood, and found worthy of relating and sharing, by another. This joy must stem from perceiving that singularly exceptional longings could also be experienced in two very distant emotional terrains. This unexpected joy could well be a sort of call. Could he try, for instance, to get lost in the unfinished painting once more, in the face of all its risks? It was a question not easily answered or, more accurately, which may necessitate more than a few responses. What happened from this point on depended on the Author, partly, and the Reader, partly, who by default agreed upon entering a humble complicity. The picture could be painted in many different manners, for instance, could be envisioned in a multitude of colors and allusions, and sustained within different stories and persons entirely. This must be one of the options of progressing in desire, that little death. In that case Hidayet might once more crave that eternal silence. Yet where in the painting would this storm, this earthquake years overdue, take him, what color, retracing of his steps, or postponed departure did it signal? The question necessitated its own question, naturally. All said and done, however, most things didn't go as desired, as we all know. A voice, disconcertingly, suddenly called Hidayet to dinner. The element of monotony must have been included as a small warning to Hidayet to not keep at this manuscript for much longer. Could one be sure enough, however, that these questions would not be transposed in a different manuscript, in another manner entirely, despite the despondency suffered on all counts?*

34
My Lie, My Captivity, a True "Bird on a Wire"

"To be honest, I don't know anymore how we can situate ourselves in this story, or at what point," said the Man, as the Author, for the sake of a little journey toward certain intricacies in such a chapter, first contemplated an outfit, then a history, and finally an era for his protagonist. By virtue of his precedency he kept the outfit and the history for himself, remembering the many possibilities that could help his advance toward a special, deeply special person. Next up was the magic and inhabitability of the archaic time frame. He thought of the story of the cool summer evenings, perceived that there were poems he could advance in for the sake of different longings entirely, feeling no discomfort, absolutely none, about the fact that many might consider the return to such an evening an amateurish obsession. He knew the magic of words, after all, he'd used them before, and he knew of the call of intricacies; for some of his friends, for example, all he had to do was to touch upon the poetry of the sea. It occurred to him then that one could hope for the scent of August for the sake of certain longings. He considered one of the houses of his fantasies for his protagonists. Here all must be suitable for evasion or captivity, the illusory beauty of Istanbul, capable of hiding all suffering, visible from the balcony at evening time, an averted gaze, abrupt gust of wind, a light blinking far, far away from behind a curtain of obscurity or the horn of a ferry ripping unexpectedly through the stillness must all in their own ways contribute to the small possibility of narrating manifold resentments. While preparing for an interview about the book, perhaps a Woman could prepare a drink for the Man as he, together with the Author, searched for his place in the book. Important clues could naturally be derived from this last sentence. The Man, for instance, could be

one of the intellectuals one is wont to come across in a myriad of familiar places, and inasmuch as his intellectuality may have been limited to reading Newsweek or the credentials of a school taught in English, having acquired the habit of having a drink before dinner was the mark of a distinct identity in itself. Whether the drink in question would be rakı or something imported was only a small matter of preference in terms of its associations. The second important clue could be identified in the presence of a woman. That the Woman was preparing the Man's drink, naturally, was significant in regard to the constitution of the relationship. No matter what the essence, affection tinged with slight intoxication, whether received or given, had completely different meaning in the lives of those who were incessantly and obligatorily running from numerous disappointments. Doubtless the roles could be exchanged without warning in order to prevent certain assaults concerning this small detail about preparing drinks or being silent. It honestly went without saying, there was no point in clouding an evening rife with the meaning of singular poetry or special sentiments with feminist/masculinist argument. The Author had, on nearly every occasion afforded to him, made his opinions clear on the subject, advocating the despicability of masculinist societies in language nowhere close to being equanimous even as certain of his peers, champions of heterosexism, appraised him as a schlep floundering in sexual misery, inadvertently causing the collapse of deeply secret fictions, despite all the poetry he'd dreamed of and tried to share in order to gain approval, by pointing out that feminism, despite its apparent righteousness, was a movement liable to fall tangent to certain fundamental problems of humanity. As it was, making sense of such attitudes was no simple matter, in these days passing by in a haze of fear and anxiety, not much was more important than this steadily waning feeling of affection; but when sexuality and the void it consistently failed to fill was in question, one easily found oneself, despite all reluctance, caught in the trap of superficial discussions. That was why possibilities were magical, that must be partly why in the midst of so much desperation and defeat, the realm of fantasy *hadn't lost its luster. Who knows, perhaps the woman in this manuscript must be a woman who, without a shred of remorse, must be favored over the multitudes who dressed casually, who were interested in the arts in the name of labels and superficiality, more attractive than most men could remain impervious to, unable, despite their casual appearances, to overlook certain subtle, old-fashioned details while greeting their guests, certainly spoke one or two foreign languages, were able to read printed matter in said languages, fond of intermittently sprinkling words from these languages amid their arty rhetoric while appearing regretful that it were their shortcomings in their native language that forced them to do so, who read* Cumhuriyet Daily *or thought it one of the most essential elements of their identity to proclaim that they did, who drank banana milk or instant coffee at fixed hours in the day and sat cross-legged on the sofa, who had had many affairs up till their relationship with this man, had tried their hands at bridge or tennis or piano or some other instrument before surrendering them to the flow of time in favor of other acquired interests, who in the meantime also had an affinity for the vegetarian diet, in short: despite all defeats and subjugations, hadn't been able to evade, due to their shortcomings, the trap of building their lives on whatever political viewpoint they found unassailable, held above all things their duty, at least at certain intervals, to their religion's requirements, whichever one it was, and maintained this attitude in the name of tradition, that lamest of concepts, believing they contributed to life in this way or that due to their work with associations, whose involvement in art was limited to the colored pages of magazines and who considered Stephen King, Harold Robbins, or Woody Allen to be writers. In this manuscript, the Author could show extra effort to refrain from defining the protagonists' marital status, in other words, allude to an "open relationship"—whatever that meant—for the sake of emphasizing a disparate kind of identity, by connection enriching this preordered décor with a quality most people would find covetable from several angles. However, as is clear from this sentence, it would be much more sensible to think of this situation*

*as a possibility, a mere possibility at this point. And while we're here,
it would behoove me to point out that this house, where we'll be
guests at least for the duration of this manuscript, has been furnished
according to the needs of the aforementioned life. By association, for
the sake of numerous images and evocations, it's natural that we
should benefit from the continuation of certain films within us.
After all, everyone has film stills they somehow keep alive in their
imaginations and adventures in numerous relationships through
which such stills are prolonged. All else aside, no matter the interval
of time, this attitude is more or less necessary in order to open up a
space of freedom, if narrow, for the persons in the process of creating
this body of text. Yet while we've been brought to the subject, some
additional explanation is required to prevent certain likely misunderstandings. There's much to be derived, for instance, from disclos-
ing the Author's great appreciation of the fact that his book had been
read by both of these people, no matter what the situation or apparent situation, and what's more, would have done anything to externalize this appreciation in the guise of a so-called show of modesty.
Glaringly incomplete in every regard, this book had certainly not
been read by a conservative civil servant who spent the majority of
his vacations in striped pajamas and had no qualms about drinking
rakı from a tea glass on picnic grounds, a neo-Nazi who spoke
Turkish, a reader of pulpy romances who appreciated fluid prose,
an anti-Semitic preacher, a columnist who considered aggression,
mere aggression, a merit, and knew his writings gave nothing to the
future, or a reptile in the guise of an intellectual. The Man's piquant
phrase of pursuit that laid bare his foray into the manuscript, however, is still thought-provoking in this regard. There seems to be a
problem in need of immediate solution, a secret in need of exposure,
an appeal that unexpectedly eggs the Author on, compelling him to
write this manuscript. It is, in other words, a line between advancing and standing still, a pause, a regret beforehand experienced, a
kind of fear, a time of wanting to leave everything as it is and
advancing toward another kind of loneliness in the face of all the
consequences. At such a moment, however, the Woman comes to the*

Author's rescue, frankly, at a rather unexpected instant, by telling the Man, "The play is woven from disappointment and resentment just as in this story, and despite all our efforts, all the limits we test in the name of bettering this life and all the details we've sought, we've been barred offstage, though the stage remains in us, and nothing will be as we longed for, as we wished for it to appear, and shall not." Barred offstage, yes. In that case there's nothing to be gained from dreaming of entering a manuscript, of living with the possibilities it's rife with, or for that matter, attempting to share something in connection to a book review through such a manuscript. Life goes on much differently, after all, for all those who agree to play the game by the rules than it does in this manuscript. Yet to tell the truth, the woman's assigned enunciation of such a phrase in this manner is also thought-provoking. This point is without a doubt related to reasons such as the Author's blatant partiality, his weakness for women of the sort, and thus his entrapment, not for the first time. The Narrator's experiences in this book are sufficiently explanatory regarding the developments of this captivity. Ultimately, the Woman's declarations are constantly uttered, albeit in different words, and discussed in such settings, no matter what the Author may obsess over. For to search for a solidarity of dubious reliability in a complaint or hurtfulness, that's one of the rare weapons left in these people's hands. The matter approached from this angle, the conditions form, or seem to form, for this book being fit for discussion, even if briefly. The die is cast once more; the Author is an observer once more, a witness to the hell of his own creation despite all his authority and opportunities. It's impossible, of course, to avoid the infinitely varying and often contradictory commentary on what's been written, seen the daylight after so much delay and worry. Why, for instance, after all the stories, has this book been written, and who in fact is this lover? This is a risky question. For the author himself, after having brought this manuscript to this point, doesn't know the answer. This is a risky question. For it brings with it the pain of desperation, an exclusion. The Author has always experienced passion in his imagination, as the so-called reflection of a certain life. This is the story, indeed, of a fantasy, a delusion. Why, then, have these people been, or hoped to be, transcribed into text? Was all this effort in the name of articulating resentment, or a nebulous attempt at self-preservation? Where, with whom, and how were these stories supposed to continue now? The Author was, in all honesty, deeply curious to see how the Man and the Woman in the manuscript would respond to these questions in their brief reverie over drinks. Yet had he not claimed in previous stories that pairing one silence with another could at times mean salvation, a means of delay in the name of connecting to the present moment, had he not insisted on the meaning of clinging to, preferring to cling to, these question marks? Such an approach naturally rendered many efforts and iterations meaningless. All aside, this book that could provide a new argument entirely to explain the seeking of sanctuary in words, mere words no matter how risky, would be placed before not too long into the bookcase in this house, to be spoken of many, many years later, this woman, who for the Author would always remain a fantasy or a possibility would say, while sipping her drink on ice and listening to Leonard Cohen's "Bird on a Wire," "I couldn't remain impervious to such an affair, I may very well have responded to such a call," attempting in vain to sound convincing, and the Man, who inwardly bore the resentment of never having permeated the text as deeply as he wished, would respond to these words with a tentative, bitter smile. Once more an opportunity had been missed, and many people carried on living around us unreceptive to all the suffering and evasion they couldn't have ignored if not for their deafened sensibilities. These were well-known, oft-processed disappointments, widely hoped to be shared. All said and done, however, as much as we turned a blind eye to certain situations and ran as fast as we could from certain words and images, we were obligated always to take on this hazardous journey certain truths and feasibilities. In other words, stories weren't ended or spent so easily. The Author wanted to imagine for his protagonists—who had no interest in this manuscript that he'd devised for the articulation of a discontent hard to define and who by extension didn't allow him to write to his heart's desire the stories, in spite of all his preparations—a feasibility and a quiet union rather than a forced parting of ways. The drinks would be finished in a little while, for example, the Man and Woman expected to head into the kitchen for dinner later still. First, however, the Man would have to remove the finished record and replace it with Vivaldi's Four Seasons. *Music must also be considered, yes, a little music to greet the night once more. A little nocturne. A little nocturne. Yet would it all be enough to articulate that never-ending inferno?*

35
Of Drinks, Evenings, and Getting Lost on the Way Home

IT WOULDN'T BE ENOUGH; of course, no inferno was finished, would not yet be spent considering the assault of words, and in the hurricane of possibilities no lives would be lived licentiously. As such the Author thought it practically an obligation to continue on his clandestine journey in this book, thinking of certain acquaintances of his who made do with hackneyed comments and others' words and thoughts, unrelentingly and tirelessly searched for negativity in what was written, and experienced all forms of criticism available to them between a pair of wineglasses and a pair of legs. It was in reality the tale of a delusion, an old, extremely old lie. The voices of those who sought their dilemmas in another attempted to bear regrets by turning them into bittersweet joys, longed for every loss in an attempt to question and increasingly preserve the past, believed in the viability of nuanced sensibility, and thought hypocrisies that could be hidden behind gleaming words, at times an honor and at times an obligation, had perhaps never been heard, or wished to be heard, in any number of evening preparations or tired dawns in these circles. What words, for instance, could elaborate the story of a dilemma, could the sound of regret be experienced, transferred over during a separation or depicted like rain? With what color, lost person, lover, or unexpressed passion did we associate the heartbreaks that we bore inside us year after year, hoping to relate to another? Should the dinner parties that after a point in the evening turned, with their worn-out rhetoric, into a nightmare, a crowded journey into loneliness, be explained by the hope for self-preservation or self-obliviousness, even if briefly? The sea was always the same sea, after all, the seasons had also been renewed years ago, the same preparations, for all we know, and the same excitement for new clothes all for the sake of the same people. Our obligations to ourselves and our imprisonment by others hadn't changed, in other words, despite new words, intoxications, and discourses, despite all our efforts. As on this tiny isle of literature or art, as on all other isles, nearly everyone was in on the game, truth be told; nearly everyone was some kind or other of partner in the crime. These were in a way the consequences of a kind of conformism where irreconcilability was played at, seemingly. Many turns of phrase could be altered without a second thought, perhaps, or ignored with just the same ease. But was the door knocked on not always the same door, the voice known to be behind it, making itself heard sporadically, not the echo of the pursuit of an identity, was it not always the expression of the same evasion that waited to encounter us somewhere? As such, there was no need to get one's hopes up once again or go chasing after expansive dreams. In this landscape where many stories marched on in deafened sensibility in nearly every relationship, this book, like others of its kind, would most likely not be read in the way its author had intended. At most there would be those who discussed the book with the scrutiny of a writer, a poet, a magazine journalist, and interpreted it in their own fashion, the rules of the game determining that there was nothing redeemable about such a story in a world containing much more serious problems. The astonishing needlessness of this chapter full of resentments difficult to identify with would then be laid upon the table, claims made as to the staggering self-indulgence that could only explain such an attitude, and that no book should ever be found to be worthy of so wanton and lengthy a discussion. No one was all that concerned with another, after all, everyone lived by their own rules and in accordance with their own stories. These inferences, however, still didn't free the Author from certain misgivings. As it was, the reasons behind the writing of the chapter were reviewed once more, were attempted to be reviewed despite the risks. Had there, for instance, been a disservice done to these people, and a measure of selfishness concerned with undertaking certain observations and attributions? Had one-dimensional, lifeless types been ultimately relayed, wishful observations rather than reality expressed with the added effect of a number of unsolved dilemmas? These questions were tantamount to a warning, and perhaps the same as a small request for an inquisition. One could, however, also venture toward a story, one whose objective was not yet apparent. That was partly the reason that the Author, taking advantage of his well-honed quality of dubious consistency, his ability to be anywhere at any time, set out on a jittery walk around the tiny isle. He stopped by libraries and briefly perambulated chain bookstores, movie theaters, concert and conference halls. He encountered many people there who took their duties seriously, perceiving that they weren't among those who constantly postponed reading in order to write. A small, bittersweet appreciation spread through him then. He went then to the bars, to the decrepit island's most favored, most alcohol-soaked restaurants. It was all under the guise of joy or a thinly veiled sadness. The extremely colorful discussions of contemporary art events along with the extremely colorful realizations of earlier sexuality-centered conversations were naturally no surprise. There were so many people around here who didn't want to return home to the system that they, in one way or another, were prisoners to. No one spoke, or even seemed to wish to any longer, of reading the whole night through, fantasies of vanishing into a book or the foolish behavior that might be tolerated for the sake of a story. All motions gained meaning through design, numerous dawns were longed for only through that, a mere design. An incessantly repeating season of solitude seemed to be underway around here, with numerous people all clamoring about taking off, shooting big-budget films, writing great poems, novels, dissertations, about great sex, great vacations, or publishing great magazines. Indeed, all was at the stage of an idea, some great scheme. At the time the Author seemed to be peering at the people who might be up to reading his book from behind several pages he felt would never be fully perceived. He wasn't really in another world, not really, and it didn't even cross his mind to take pride in his nonconformity and alienation. Perhaps the problem stemmed from the dramatization and over-idealization of a myriad of longings, sentiments, and lifestyles in spite of all the disappointments they brought. This attitude necessitated some small measure of anger, a kind of resentment against the self, and laid a new and treacherous groundwork for certain kinds of defeat. He knew very well by now how this story would progress, as well as, for that matter, how it would end. It didn't matter how much one thought about others, as a matter of fact, nor, in other words, did playing with fire. He considered then that he might return once more to his isolation at his writing desk, thinking of the peerless enchantment of the music/literature dichotomy and the meaning of songs that remained and would remain unchanged in spite of the far, faraway lands. "Would you be willing to rewrite this strange song over again in another way?" he asked suddenly. No one replied. "Understood, understood, all is in place, everything is on the right track," he said at that. He thought of Selami on the way back. "I must absolutely remember to send Selami to that bookstore," he said to himself, thinking it was best not to mention this to anyone, "thank heaven for these games," he said, too, "thank heaven for these games." But those who knew Selami knew well, also, of his honesty and candidness, he was widely described as a trustworthy friend and for that matter a real solid guy all around. Yet those who knew him knew, too, how headstrong he could be, how unexpectedly resistant he was, at times, to phrases offered to him, and how utterly plastered he could manage to get at times of no one's convenience. With such characteristics he might unpredictably vanish soon after accepting this request, causing everything to grind to a halt midway, and more importantly, the unexpected annihilation of numerous symbols pertaining to that old story. Still, it was an adventure worth undertaking despite all its hazards. It was then that the Author contemplated once more the attitude his protagonist might affect in the face of certain events or people. He smiled. "Come on then, Selami," he said abruptly, "come now and let's meet once more like in those delightful old days at our writing table for the sake of a quiet preparation. Perhaps together we may set out on the adventure of a brand-new story. Even if we achieve nothing, at least we'll come away with this fleeting meeting, this little pursuit of entertainment and our awakening to new questions." The Author glanced around, a little nervously, at the completely empty street. It seemed that no one had heard him. All must be in order, solitudes and the forced retracing of steps all on track.

36
If You Only Knew Why Selami Disappeared

WHEN HE RECEIVED THE request, Selami in truth had understood very well what was expected of him. It was the kind of power derived from having lived with his author year after year and shared with him, and more importantly ventured into along with him, the multitudes of words, lovers, and possibilities, an anticipated expression of an unshowy, beautifully self-contained sense of solidarity. When he received the request, during an hour of solitude, Selami had been trying to extract brand-new stories for himself out of the deaths, births, and streets between the dusty books at the civil registry office, musing about heaven-knows-what lies, what stories and bizarre sentences his author would glean from these books if he were to come here. Muse as he did, however, he also couldn't stop worrying that his author wouldn't easily find in himself the strength to visit this place again, that of late he'd become a little too preoccupied with certain strange people, stories, and voyage preparations, and that such preoccupation, despite its apparent negligence, may well carry risks such as suicide, aneurysm, insanity or eczema. He thus decided against going further, at least at this point, sensing that problems stemming from paying excessive attention to details tailored to sentences he deeply disliked or that his author insisted on overlooking already weighed on his mind enough. This decision, of course, was not due to having lost his interest in the events, as fictional characters didn't age or change climates or lives unless their authors wished it. Yet the lovingly created Selami from the story written once-upon-a-time, and published in spite of all obstacles, was obliged, in the name of underscoring inevitability, to assume such an attitude, in other words a sudden renunciation, no matter if he wanted to or not. The resentment of being unable to do *anything other than uphold rules or an entirely different union in spite of everything: this tiny adventure must be endeavored now, and naturally this appeal from an old friend responded to. It was because of this that Selami strolled so blithely out of that old story. Putting on his shades, he checked that his pens and the pieces of paper on which he'd scribble down the first drafts of the notes he would transcribe into his logbook were in the right inside pocket of his jacket. He then imagined himself at the door of one of the most famous bookstores in the city. Bypassing obstructions such as traffic, the scent of women, the rudeness of cabdrivers, and the enormous zoo-like crowd of people, his author helped this old protagonist of his, for this old manuscript's sake, risking a flurry of criticism, by whipping events together in one long sentence and allowing the trip, if in a somewhat unseemly manner, to continue on from the door of the bookstore. A surprising crowd had gathered here for some reason, with a multitude of people seemingly taking an interest in postcards, videocassettes containing sociopolitical messages, and crepe paper. For Selami, naturally, this was a reason for fury, melancholy, for an expected itch. Rather than falling straight into hopelessness, however, he briefly examined the faces of those who appeared capable of interpreting the present through the lens of books on political analysis, in the tradition of his old, very old habit, tried to imitate the clandestine and coy fervor of the statuesque ladies who managed to prove their intellectualism by toting around the most recent and bestselling books and flashing their front covers to anyone who crossed their path, and murmured to himself, though well aware that he might make certain people angry and, more importantly, overshadow the beneficial relationships built in the name of sales or publicity with his remarks for no good reason, that even the dead in the civil register lived much better than these people. That was the moment, just as he was gearing up to agitate, that he came across the latest book by his author. The book was displayed in the new publications section. He lingered there for a longish while, acting as though he was interested in several books. His real purpose, of course, was to observe those taking an interest in his author's book. It didn't work out as he expected, however; there was such lack of interest in the book that he never had to reach for his pens and the scraps of paper. Blushing slightly and risking being recognized for no practical reason, he approached the Bookseller, who on this Saturday morning was outwardly enjoying selling sheaves of crepe paper and books on political analysis, and asked him whether Mario Levi's* Our Best Love Story *had been selling well as of late. Taken aback and slightly unnerved, the Bookseller in any case composed himself quickly enough to reply, "I've heard of neither that author nor that book until today," as he wiped dust off the books he thought he knew well. "I'll bury you, boy," thought Selami, while saying out loud rather sharply, "Come, sir, come and let's take a small world tour around your bookstore." Once more the Bookseller was taken aback and once more unnerved, assuming himself to be face-to-face with a lunatic, though also not ruling out the possibility that this bizarre person might be police. Selami brought the Bookseller over to the new publications section and pointed to his author's book, demanding, "What do you say to that, sir?" "Nothing, sir, nothing," replied the Bookseller, rather insolently, "it's just that, of the new publications, the political ones have been selling a little better recently, is all." "No harm done, then," said Selami unperturbedly, "no harm done at all, but will you have no trouble explaining, in the simplest of terms, the obvious presence of the book here of the author you just claimed not to recognize?" "I understand sir, I understand very well," the Bookseller replied in turn, he had no doubts now about Selami's complete lunacy. For the book being mentioned, or being hustled into existence, wasn't there, it was nowhere and had never been, and to top it off, the Bookseller, as a bookseller of many years, was sure of it. Did they have a book-ucination on their hands? In other words, was Selami the only person who could see this book, were there tales that took on form or played out only in lives of his sort? Selami took in once more the Bookseller and said, somewhat crest-fallen, "Defeat is defeat anywhere." The Bookseller, still taking care to err on the side of caution and decorum, said, "If you leave me your name, I may call you one day. I feel inclined, for some reason,* to believe what you say, to join in your enthusiasm. You never know, someday I just might come across this author of yours." But Selami knew very well where to draw the line. He'd had a massive argument with his author in determining this very aspect of his character in the preparatory stage of that story written long ago, making the decision, at one point, to opt out of the game, in other words, to refuse to participate in the story, but both sides had ultimately known to compromise for certain concessions and certain longings just like everyone that abides living with another. That was why he made sure to thank the Bookseller profusely for his time. "The day comes," he said, "when, at a time you least hope for or expect, certain truths surface like slaps to the face. You comprehend, suddenly, that you're situated inside a fantasy. I'll wait eagerly for the day you call, of course. There's no need to give you my address. Just keep me in your mind as you wish. My name is Selami. It will all be clearer once you discover the necessary trace. Lastly, a friendly suggestion: don't be afraid of searching between the lines, in your own fashion, for unwritten sentences and secret parentheses." Selami had reached the door of the store as he said these last words. As he exited the story, he'd reached an agreement with his author. He would head toward a new manuscript, hazarding the dangers, in the name of an age-old friendship and a pursuit, the longing to find an answer to an imprudent question, no matter how unsubstantiated, and though he'd be entirely free in terms of setting and time frame, in order not to put certain people in a difficult position and more importantly, in order not to lose his identity, for no reason at that, he would certainly return to where he belonged someday. All said and done, he needed some time just now. That was part of the reason why, as a privileged protagonist, he longed to wander through the city's streets at length, taking in all the minute details that might prove to be important. "As a matter of fact, the events happening here might also make for a story," he thought then. He smiled, noticing that he'd begun to perceive and process certain situations in the vein of his author. It was only natural that one we spent decades with left traces of himself within us, that we could advance toward the same person together.

Selami was imbued with a familiar sense of melancholy, which, who knows, may have been why he wished to stop by that park he hadn't been to in so long, in spite of his apprehensions. That the park, these benches, this sound of rustling leaves were all imaginary had little significance at this point. He was thoroughly practiced, after all his experiences, in using certain of his privileges. He could, for example, ask his author about the narrative of such a departure, something along the lines of, "Don't we all live in a fantasy, or have in the past?" In one of these imaginary sentences he dwelled on the tendrils of this caustic affair extending inside this story, on the painter Hidayet, who was spent a little more each day by drink and by that painting that wouldn't loose its grip on him, that man and woman and those odd writers who lived inside the vicious cycle of minor pleasures and the minor annihilation of minor longings. Everything was a dream, or could be explained by a dream, yes. That book, the book titled Our Best Love Story, *for instance, had never existed or been written to the heart's content. Selami was too sensitive and thoughtful to tell his author that, however. "What dreams are saved by small lies," he said to himself instead, musing on his way back that pretending nothing was wrong could be a small act of rebellion, a silent resistance. The story was always the same story, after all, and words and melancholy transferred from one to another in always the same way, always the same desperation. Selami felt a little disheartened by this, thinking to himself that, no matter what, he'd never be able to abide this behavior, this habit of living, and these compromises. His insides were suffused by bittersweet joy, a kind of melancholy he'd always had trouble expressing. The return was to square one and the story was the same, in other words. The real problem would begin in starting to relate this story to the Author in all its clarity.*

37
Do We Believe This Woman?

THE LOVER THOUGHT THEN, *"Everything goes around and comes around only to get tangled up in a wounding phrase, full of associations and without hope of return," asking herself whether she could bear such weight within as she moved onto other people and hopes and different love affairs entirely. In her new solitude she made coffee for herself on the stove and gazed at the stars that in her many resentments she was accustomed to seeing from the window of her room, in the name of an intricate detail or a possible sense of symmetry of questionable necessity. She would spend this night away from her lover, who was entirely unaware of all that had transpired, living out this book in a dissimilar way. She then thought, as if in a dream, of all the words and images she couldn't express, which filled her partly with frustration and partly with a kind of melancholy that tasted of desperation. The insistent call was right beside her now with all its associations and unaccountability. She peered at the book she was holding a while longer. How quickly it had all begun, progressed, and ended, and what a singular, incommunicable adventure or vision of time endeavored. Where was the Narrator now, who, long before this book, had sprung from one of those stories written for the sake of different longings and resentments entirely, crossing her path on a night like this and entering her life at a moment she was utterly unprepared for to call her to a possibly beautiful journey to a faraway place, to the adventure of a brand-new story, on what journey of hope, of solitude had he set out, what words had enticed him after all the disenchantments? Could they unite once more and in time come to see it all through new eyes? In the far distant future, could this story be written in a fashion utterly different than it had been today?*

Would everyone keep living, as in almost every relationship that ends, tapering off despite all wishes to the contrary, in their own way, with their own hopelessness and trivial dreams? Or, in reality, were all these lives, joys, and endearments just a rather unconscious progression into a delusion, increasingly a hallucination? In such a story, to what extent were their words, dreams, and resentments real, and to what extent mere possibility? Was it all a sleep paralysis that permeated life more and more with each day, and from which there was no waking? Yet if it were so, if it really were so, how to explain these pangs and these perilous narrative preparations? She'd merely wished to be able to express, during the time when that long, persistent call turned with each passing day into navel-gazing, an introversion and, who knows, perhaps, a self-harboring, that despite all hopes and longings all that transpired here was just a dream, to tell this fact as best as she could; she had wished to explain that no love affair could be lived out the way the Narrator hoped, that no prospective lover would take the step toward such a dream. She didn't exist in the way the Narrator had hoped for, in other words, and as long as this passion, these inevitable discords and obligatory suffering continued to exist, she never would in spite of all the rhetoric and pursuits. Ways were parted due to misunderstandings and untimeliness, yes. Yet did understanding really exist in human relationships at all; did timeliness exist? Such questions were wont now to lead her to the misgivings of a pursuit that she was in no way prepared to face, where she might find her reflection, increasingly her ghost, in these words and these resentments. "Despite everything, whether I want to or not, I have to bear this burden," she said to herself, "I have to carry the pain of this passion within me as I live, no matter how many years pass." These reflections gave her the courage to open the book once more, she considered her identity as a researcher and writer: she might do a review of the book with the help of a treasured publisher friend, in its guise replying to the distant call in well-chosen sentences and speaking to the Narrator of his aforementioned realizations, resentments, and anxieties; in other words, she could go as far as to write the story of a story. This would perhaps turn out to be a journey where the Narrator would agree to venture into a brand-new dilemma or relationship in an utterly dissimilar manuscript in spite of his complete lack of zeal. To go on an obligatory voyage in a manuscript. It was one of the Narrator's oft-attempted causeries. At that moment melancholy and a bittersweet joy appeared to infuse her very being. She smiled, thinking of how all these experiences would remain unknown to anyone else, and would be found unbelievable even if they weren't. Yet to tell the truth, none of that mattered, or shouldn't, considering the persistence of certain songs within our own selves. For minor dreams and minor stories had always been present in our lives, and we'd persist in living, in wanting to live, what we had kept hidden to ourselves for as long as separations, disappointments, and unwarranted melancholy were with us, we would always wish to maintain the secrecy. Words, words, words: had the magic of this call, these anxieties, not been enunciated years, even centuries ago? It was an evening around then, yes. It was only the most fitting time for melancholy, for the song of homecoming. What had transpired had transpired, what had been written, written once more. She discovered herself as such in the mirror of time, of a probable and inconvenient solitude, and thought that she too might be able to stand in front of it with new words and memories. She was in fact not at all the tall, red-haired, blue-eyed, full-lipped woman the Narrator had depicted and talked about, she was a local in the old Istanbul district but, despite her incessant searching, had never found the island. Ultimately some passions were lived out not as they ought to have been, but as they were dreamed of. All aside, no image reflected another image fully enough, and never would. It felt as though somewhere, always, would be hidden the dregs of unanswered questions, the remnants of an absence. The dregs of unanswered questions, yes. He was no stranger to these words either. They signaled the perpetuation of the game in spite of everything. In that case, instead of being a lover who declined or was unable to reply to a call, she was allowed to envisage herself as a woman who had lived with the Narrator for fifteen years, as alive in her flesh and blood as anything else, and thus unable to understand the reason for the writing of such a story as this, who at times liked what was written in the book and at others, didn't, who bathed and made love like anyone else and on top of it all, shopped like anyone else, helping this manuscript, increasingly a book, to be designed in a completely different way altogether. Anything could become metamorphosed, transform after its own fashion as long as one carried on dreaming. Yet didn't this thought in itself mean captivity, a compulsory withdrawing into oneself?

38
New Loves, New Disappointments

NOW, AT THIS TIME that all is close to returning once more to its own closed-off isolation, and somewhere far beyond the hopes bound to absence, I must rethink, share with you, and write down, as unbelievable as many will find it, this story of a love affair that has been forced upon me against my wishes, that I'm somehow obligated to assemble, interpret, examine, shape, and, who knows, perhaps to finish. To call a friend whose presence you're sure of, a possible lover, to a long, long story, in full awareness of its irresponsiveness, of an inevitable isolation and a lethal adventure that you're likely to have trouble relating or defining. This must be a dangerous trap, a trap that in my opinion aptly illustrates the dilemma faced by the Narrator. To write a sentence together, however, or if not, to breathe it together, at least, this inevitable complicity must sooner or later be afforded. As such, a question might descend upon our lives out of nowhere, a question that, in connection to the relationships we may have had in the past, may give rise to entirely new evocations: who is really the defeated party in such love affairs, the one whose love is unrequited or the one who is unable to reply to love with a single "I love you"? We're once more faced with one of the questions difficult to answer, difficult to transfer to another or to an obligatory isolation. It's an unchanging trajectory, really, it's our reason for becoming attached to a person. At times like these you find yourself suddenly stalled somewhere, perceiving that the burden you're forced to bear is tantamount to your dream vagabondage. You are trailed once more by the resentment of the untold. It's in that instant that the dream you set out in search of collapses: an instant that confronts you with the sudden vision of a poem, a song, or two unfamiliar lovers flashing in your eyes, that leaves you afraid to repeat yourself and the past. You can no longer tell what lie is being told through this song, poem, or vision. Yet at times like these you're also swept away into an altogether new kind of destruction by not being part of the illusory joy of that lie. Are loves in those stories then merely constructed, does the lover mean to tell you that, just like in this prolonged manuscript, she will content herself with merely observing you and that she'll never come into your life? You're now left alone with this small hope and many past errors, and a bittersweet joy suddenly suffuses your being, taking you completely by surprise. An outfit hangs in the closet that's been waiting there for you, for this very day. To live or die. There's that enchanted turn of phrase that bears the age-old wound to these days in which you cannot stop searching for its meaning. To live or die, to stay or leave, yes. You really have no hope of escape other than starting all over again. That ancient song that tells you that new loves mean new disappointments rings right then in your ear. You smile. Love and relationships, we're in the same place again after all these years, but this game simply must be played, you say to yourself. You smile. Many would know, many old friends would understand the meaning of this smile of yours. A new love, a new disappointment. Are these actually enough to prepare for bittersweet joy or a new lover?

39
Epilogue, or After a Delayed Visit

(AT ONE TIME, IT seems, I had striven to journey in a manuscript, to try, try, and try novel words. I knew it was just a fancy, that the lover invited to the manuscript was a fancy, the words, the nights, the cities and towns stopped in were fancies, and it was a fancy to live out that story, to conclude it to my heart's content, and to vanish without a word into a new manuscript and land entirely.[1] In spite of any and all longings or preparations, stories simply never ended, because a sentence that lived continually in our isolation and within us, constantly resisting being written, couldn't find its place amongst our desires or be relayed to our heart's content to a lover, no matter how many hangovers and attempts at finding ourselves we weathered.[2] Around here appeared to be something that wasn't working, something hard to define, and you were running down a road we didn't know how to get to, or where it would lead, toward a strip of coast, a downpour, a street where the people seemed off-putting, capable of changing our lives at an unexpected moment. Every word, every night, every song was a fancy, yes. You were once more face-to-face with yourself, by yourself, in a place you constantly evaded defining. At a time you may want to uninhibitedly share the giddiness of a prospective beginning with your prospective loved ones, you may once again try your hand at a story you know you won't complete, abruptly coming to comprehend the many sufferings and disappointments you've been inadvertently turning a blind eye to and the many longings you forcibly delayed and, who knows, perhaps then you may resist returning to the past, to the matchless enchantment of departures.[3] After all, as always, downright dangerous evocations would be involved, liable to drag you kicking and screaming into certain dilemmas you were steadfast about hiding.[4] That was partly why you must review your feasible self-defenses at every step you may take, at every punctuation mark you come across, between every pair of parentheses, and every probable association of every word you choose; you mustn't find yourself having to make clarifications at unexpected times and in unexpected ways. A risky and thus rather unnerving start was in question, yes. Yet on those days, no matter what the outcome, despite all my apprehensions or resentments, as always, I had set out on the pursuit of certain choices that at first wouldn't be easy to define, I saw that much more clearly now, and more importantly, I could say it. To set out in pursuit of choices. It was an expansion that merited fastening upon, that also incited somewhat of feeling of peace toward various forms of living. At such times, for instance, in the name of evocations that could return to us with different meanings entirely, I would imagine what may have happened in a tiny room, I'd look back on the books abandoned in one of the turns of phrase, uncompleted, the neglected journeys, the unquenched sensualities, the untold dreams, and how you may always and constantly need access to certain words and images. Then it was time for another story, for a longing for another life. It may have been feasible to live with unfinished books, relationships, or songs, certain appeals were necessary, it seems, to be birthed into pain, unprompted, to stay in a region woven out of sorrow, consolations, and dangerous expectations, to be a person who, through forced grins, changed a little bit more, and reluctantly, with each passing day.[5] Rooms, beds, and lives I hide inside myself with their tens of thousands of associations. Silence. A fine line between sleep and wakefulness on long, long nights in spite of thorough inebriation, a vast,

deep, silent, indeterminate wait.[6] These were the visions of
an evasion, of an age-old daydream, to be perfectly honest.
All aside, I had once set out on a journey that for some reason had always resisted being narrated. Advancing in words,
I had said to myself, while a night pooled inside of me com-
prised of loneliness, symbols, and deceitful sex. Perhaps it
was this night I had dreamed of relating an old, age-old story
and its traces left in me that I had hoped to relive once more
in the face of all its risks.[7]

"You'll be comfortable here," said the Old Woman, "it's
the largest room of our bed-and-breakfast, *and* it overlooks
the garden. So the noise from the street won't wake you
too early in the morning. All you have to do to turn on
the radiator is press this button. There's an extra blanket in
the closet if you need it. The bathroom's down the hall on
the right. You must be tired from the road, you may want
to take a bath. Breakfast is between 7:30 and 8:30 in the
morning. See to it that you're not late. And don't forget to
lock your door before you go to sleep. If you'd like to go
outside at night, let me know and I'll give you the keys to
the outer door. You can also ring the bell, though, I don't
sleep much anyhow. Not that there's much to see around
this city, the people aren't that fond of visitors, and to boot,
everyone lives in their own isolations, as everywhere else;
they can't tell anyone, but you know."[8] Are these words a
signal that this long spiel is drawing to a close? I know it
would make things much, much easier if we didn't have to
linger so long on meanings that tie in with irresolution. All
said and done, however, no problem was ever solved through
words as thoroughly as initially planned, nor can it ever
be. That's part of the reason why the rules of this journey
must be taken to heart. The question of how words live on
in other stories alongside other words, on the other hand, I
suppose we can only answer through other stories.[9] I look at
the Old Woman walking down the hall. Her shuffling steps,

wheezing, coughing, and the cigarette she perpetually seems to have in her hand bring to mind certain film stills I can't at this time place. A cat approaches her then, seeking attention, it rubs against her ankles and meows as though to tell her something. From its languorous movements I can tell that it, too, is quite elderly. In recollection of a friendship in a novel I read ages, even eons ago, I think that they might be sharing one of their own; a difficult-to-define, so to say, deeply special friendship. She turns on her way down the stairs as though sensing that she was being watched and says, "It's time for her dinner," as though enunciating a resentment given meaning through affection, or a resignation to cohabitation. "The older she gets, the crankier and less patient, as though she were afraid of being left hungry . . . anyhow, you had better get some rest. You're pale, and you look quite tired and drained, too."[10] I shut the door.[11] I turn on the light at my bedside and stretch out on the bed. The sounds then drift in of the woman talking to the cat in a language I have difficulty identifying. I ask myself once more why I came here, why I wished so badly to see this room and depict it, I'm reminded of the appeal of the thousands of stories and novels that gave my life direction in a myriad of ways up to this day.[12] But then no matter how hard I try I can't be sure that I really experienced this place in the ways I've tried to depict and assumed myself to have seen it up till this point, can't explain to my heart's content what prolonged story I should dwell here for the sake of. I can only claim that there was a dream. But after what shortfalls and defeats had the dream begun? These are clearly dangerous questions for a night or an isolation such as this. I try to forget, to chase after familiar dreams so I can evade my own self and certain ghosts. Then I ponder what I almost always ponder in a place such as this. I wonder about those who may have lain on this bed before me, for instance, and try to scrutinize in my own way all the things one can't tell a lover in bed, about postponed affairs, hopes, details, the bewitchment of forbidden sex, and all the aloneness to be found here; to diversify it if in some small way.[13] Then I hope that this journey will be the last one I have to set out on by myself, I wish for the transformation of this long silence into a startling cry someday soon. I feel weighed down. Within me grows, once more, the joy of the prospect of moving onto another world, if tenuous, entirely. I almost hear or merely feel the sound of the wind blowing against the window.

A room, however, no matter what its shape or evocations, was also simultaneously an expression of captivity and seeking refuge in oneself. In all the houses, apartment buildings, or the streets on and along which I lived, as with possibly all the climates of the earth, on that terrain only relatable if thoroughly experienced, certain people dreamed of, sensed, and unremittingly committed to paper, canvas or another kind of isolation entirely more or less the same things.[14] Certain predicaments had to do with small separations and various backtrackings. It was a dream being depicted, old, its colors spent in every way; it may have been a vicious cycle of a higher order, but it was a vicious cycle nevertheless. A vicious cycle that would be encountered sooner or later by anyone who had a sentiment, a story, or a resistance to tell, no matter what shape or form. After all, in our lives were obligatory slumbers, omissions, wanton evasions, numerous affordances of brand-new illusions, awakenings to so-called fresh mornings wide open to variability, musings or assumed musings, the inability to distinguish the enchantment of the night due to quotidian worries and enterprises, sounds, sounds, sounds, the apprehension of heading, always heading toward the dead, sex that after a certain while turned into, say, almost a task, an escape, and further a way of covering up shortfalls and evading certain lies, muteness, entrapments in one's own or another's silences, followed by a tiny rebellion, a strange, prolonged autumn that repeated itself constantly, words, words, words, mirrors with the foil flaking off, images that, lost, or seemingly lost, appeared before us unbidden, at unexpected times, taking us off guard. Images, yes, the endlessness of images and their never-ending stories. Those were the nights, I remember, that I struggled within my own means to give new meaning to so-called novel words.[15] The unparalleled silence of the night in that house, opening to solitude, the sound of wheezing, small, sudden shrieks piercing the stillness, the joy of being free, in some way or another, in one's sleep . . . At such small hours of the night, my grandmother would say, "It's late, go to bed now, you can carry on with your reading tomorrow," the clock on the wall would tick, and I would envisage a lover far, far away, in prospective beds making prospective love. I was progressing toward a narrative, I know. Yet what possibility was I knocking on the door of and what tiny death or disappointment awaited me behind it? That was the thing I couldn't perceive clearly enough, or relate in spite of all my longing and preparations.[16]

"Very few people can immerse themselves, in the true sense, in the particular magic of this city," the Old Waiter says. "In the beginning it has an appeal, how can I put this, extraordinary, a little difficult to explain. In a very short time, however, something seems to push you away, to abandon you. Certain images close in on themselves. And that's when you realize you won't be able to communicate with this city, not in any real sense. The houses, streets, pavements, coffeehouses, the sky, all these alienating smells and people draw away from you as much as you'd like to prevent that from happening. In other, oft-used words, the city doesn't reveal itself after a certain point. If you were merely interested in seeing miracles or historical structures, of course, there's no problem. In that case you can take the beaten track of the temporary wanderer and then, before you've seen much, head off toward other cities, people or lands with

inexplicable lure, bearing the illusion with you always. More
than that, however, would be dangerous. Further, there's a
chance that this journey might take you on a completely
dissimilar, who knows, a real journey you're likely utterly
unprepared for; it might, if you should also see fit, sweep
you off into the enclaves and increasingly the dungeons of
an adventure I know well or, at the very least, am quite sure
I know well in the light of all that I've gone through. It's a
departure, somehow always delayed, to a destination that
has no return, it's time to push the limit of certain visions
and scrutinize their side meanings after one's own fashion. If
you're able to discover a variety of meanings, so to speak, in
the smallest hours of the night, in the gait of a woman who
no sooner appears on the corner than disappears, in its echo
on this stark, utterly empty street, in the sound of a piano
drifting out from an old, decrepit, increasingly atrophying
restaurant, or in the alienating smell of a meal, find a variety
of meanings, you ought to have quite a few experiences. The
city will live on in you even if you leave. No matter where
you've gone or are going, you have become a sort of native
to the city. All else aside, after such a trip, you've left something behind whether you wished to or not. To find this
something, to better describe it, to fill the emptiness inside
you, you'll want to return here again. The longing will chase
you year after year, nightmarishly, it could even be said.
If you could only know what a long time remained until
the mystery can be solved, how difficult and inescapable
it all is, if you could only understand how it all resembles
our voyage to a person, a lover. Within your own means,
you try to relate this adventure to your own isolation or the
imperceptible faces from your past. The city awaits you, a
little as though it's a loyal lover. The city where you grew
up, that has most likely made you who you are, and others .
. . your faraway or immediate choices . . . your selves, split,
shattered, left behind in a variety of ways, with your losses

but also with your gains . . . I sense that you can identify with this story, and more, that you're living it out, right this minute."[18]

I comprehend more clearly the things that may have brought me here to this distant and partly imaginary land. It's a trap, I say to myself, the early hours of a trap I recognize from previous assays, the repercussions of which I can one way or another guess at. I feel I can understand, too, in my own way, my reasons for heading both excitedly and apprehensively toward this gigantic square or, as pointed out in the handbook I'm perusing on the way, the "City Square," at this hour of the evening. All is all right, then, nothing is as alienating as I had first sensed at the beginning of this trip. An adventure, that which resembles what the Old Waiter has tried to convey, always engulfs us in the same way in spite of all our pursuits and efforts. It's important, and very soothing, to be aware at this point of this truth. In such situations we feel too sophisticated to seek refuge in delusion.[19] Still, the words of the Old Waiter that in transcribing I've inadvertently altered send a shiver through me. It's another dimension of contradiction, a moment of eternity that renders self-assurances ineffectual, a shiver that's tantamount to a sensation of death that I try to avoid at all costs, then. Perhaps that's why I'm reticent of rampantly expressing certain emotions, thinking to myself that at this stage, silence is redemption, a seeking of refuge in oneself, and I content myself with asking the person who is ready to share this brief life with me why he has bothered to make these clarifications. "Because of the way you take notes on the handbook, because of your rather skeptical glancing around, and, perhaps, because I sense that you're tracking down a story you fear you may never complete," he replies. "You remind me of one who came here many, many years ago, with similar notions. The longing to leave, to depart to another life, that most of us keep alive only in dreams, knowing that sooner or later one is bound to be moored, forever imprisoned, somewhere. Many emotions become much clearer, make sense in time." "So what happened to that person?" I ask in turn. I feel like this is the only question that will elicit the most truthful, direct answer from the Old Waiter. The mystery seems liable to draw me to itself further. With the airs of one who is deeply accustomed to his surroundings, the loneliness that gains meaning through the appearance of the square at varying hours and its familiar faces, he says, "To stay or to leave, in a protracted, dangerous journey, our inevitable defeats in the face of certain longings and people." A brief but deeply meaningful silence divides our conversation. "There was a story that I began years ago but never completed, if you must know the truth, a story I always avoided completing," I say. "At one point in my examination was the dream of reaching toward a lover in words, and only in words. I had been invited, out of the blue, to a game. Yet somehow, in time, certain things seemed to slip through my fingers and things inexplicably spiraled out of my control. As with most affairs, it had become natural for this story to be completed or to be changed by others, continuing by constantly proliferating its options. I had become a victim of my own little game. It was the rebellion, so to speak, of possibilities. All that was left to do was to somehow carry on on the last legs of my long journey. In my long journey amongst words I could live out my own exile, my own shortcomings and my own disappointments, only for myself. Living out my own exile, yes. For the city I was born in, spoke the language and drank the water of, and wantonly perused the sea of in every way, draws further away from me with each passing day. I always felt the same resentment toward this city and others, and increasingly, also in my journeys toward other people; I always tried to resign myself to this constantly repeating disappointment. Now, for some reason, I declare it the time to retrace my steps once more. Time to return once more to that city, lover, and to those words. Yet in this retracing of steps I mention so often, I can't tell, for the life of me, whether this, my bittersweet joy, is kindled by my anticipation of meeting certain people and phrases of the past or by my improved attunement to the outcomes of certain desperations. For this story is no longer that same old story, naturally, the lover was never enjoyed in the way she was meant to, words were always treacherous, the streets were forever being lost, and I feel extraordinarily uncomfortable having to depict the sea once more, to reconstruct it in all its estrangement from me, outright struggling to express this resentment to my heart's content, and most important of all, in spite of everything, I can't say why it occurred to me to write this chapter for the sake of continuing the story, or how to associate what is portrayed here with what occurred there. To progress must be the answer, it seems, against all odds. Emotions and evocations may well lead us to an exit door we can't as yet glimpse." Upon these words the Old Waiter smiles. "The fact that you require the help of your protagonist to continue with your story is probably the most significant mark of your desperation," he says, "but seeing as we're in this together now, let's try after our own fashion to seek an answer to this drawn-out question. At some point in this manuscript, as you'll remember, I had used a turn of phrase concerning staying or leaving and the obligatory, irrevocable defeats of a never-ending, perilous journey in the face of certain longings and people. Certain clues, in my opinion, must be enmeshed here, those who are willing to listen to us should be allowed to some extent to interpret the pursuit of their discovery. Our silence, you'll also remember, was divided by silence. That in itself, I think, also carries blatant meaning. But it's best if you say nothing after it. At that stage I should've been able to change the subject or suggest a bed-and-breakfast to help relate certain sentiments

better. Here are a few sample phrases: I can suggest a bed-
and-breakfast in the city where you'll be comfortable. It's
owned by an old woman, an old, old friend, the protagonist of another, special story in itself. For years she's been
living with her cat and with memories that she's willing to
share with very few people. She doesn't welcome any old person into her home. If you told her I sent you, however, and
especially if you told her about our conversation, she should
be happy to host you." The experiences that may have happened or will happen in the room of a bed-and-breakfast . . .
can we thus put together the parts of a fragmentation and,
in this self-transcribing story, move past the call of shadows
toward an unexpected manuscript?

Such an obligatory escape was bound to yield even more
interviews than originally thought. That a body of text, a
sum of words, was seen as a sanctuary was doubtless due
to the influence of age-old stories. Age-old stories, age-old
rooms, age-old places, and affairs no one would ever live
in or endure again. In the silent storm of elicitations, there
was no doubt that different choices, identities, and affairs
could be found, provided one was willing to take the chance.
Shortfalls could be compensated for, words reconsidered,
unexpected manuscripts uncovered unremittingly, perhaps,
through lies and duplicity. The appeal of leaving things
incomplete could be partly explained thus. There's no point,
however, in repeating that easy solutions and journeys from
which we have no choice but to return can never redeem us
in any real sense. We can't easily break free of the prolon-
gation of our dreams and the fortuities within us, we can't
easily shake them off, no matter what hopes we may wield.
As much as we fall mute, seeking refuge in silence, trying
to deceive one another in various ways, we'll continue to
sense on certain nights that a conversation, one we cannot
name for the life of us, still carries on inside us. A sound, one
we're no stranger to, one we've heard time and time again in

entirely different conversations in entirely dissimilar manuscripts, one that's immersive and lives on in a person to
whom we cannot confess our affection, is bound to call back
to us at times like these whether we want to hear it or not.[20]

I'm then startled by a thump the source of which I can't
locate. I realize I must have dozed off for all of an hour. A
brief but bottomless nap; immense, so to speak. Feeling my
heart rate pick up speed, I listen for the surrounding sounds
as I try to orient myself to this sudden state of wakefulness.
Was I until an instant ago inside a dream of which no detail
or image I can seem to recall now, or in this room, half-
awake? Did someone really knock on the door? Or could
everything be explained by the fact that a delusion determined each detail you believed yourself to be experiencing?
I falter. I seem to be frozen stiff. Yet I hear nothing but
deep, discomfiting silence. I should go in the bathroom and
shower, I think. I open the door, for some reason taking care
not to make noise. From downstairs come the unfamiliar
smells of cooking and familiar sounds of dinner preparation.
That's why I murmur to myself that I know these preparations, these sounds, the things one would like to say at
such times but can't. A dim, pale light trickles out of a room
close to the middle of the hallway, I realize I'll have to walk
past it to reach the bathroom. The hardwood creaking below
my feet, underneath the worn carpet, harmonizes with the
age-old decrepitude of my surroundings, lending a different
meaning entirely to the deep sense of solitude. In front of
the door, in my understandable state, I pause briefly. I find
myself confronted at that instant with the frozen reflection
of a woman in the mirror as she stands with her back to
the door. I'm startled. The enchantment of an ancient tale
engulfs me at a moment I least expect. I know this face, and
its meaning, so well, I say to myself. Long, red hair, rich
blue eyes, and full lips . . . at that I recall once more the
story that contains an affair of another kind entirely, that

most would find unconvincing, in which a delusion, sure to result in chagrin, is afforded against all odds; incomplete and apparently never to be complete. I have trouble making sense of being confronted by this apparition at such an unexpected time. Nebulous words and resentments merely appear beside me: it was always the tale of the same dream, the same retracing of steps. I was overtaken by a sense of melancholy, a parting of ways I'm no stranger to, and the joy of setting off to an island. The song I was sure was coming from you, however, seemed to be drawing closer despite everything, penetrating me. For me this was a brand-new attempt at self-repetition, one that gained meaning through error and contradiction, the effort to track down, once more, an unreliable kind of bliss. It had been years since I learned to live with words, tales, and illusions. I thought you might be able to understand sooner or later that I had set out on this path for your sake. I knew very well, too, this surrender. The defeats, silences, and those long-standing deceptions no longer mattered. Perhaps I would bear the story of that island into brand-new relationships and possibilities. To greet the night . . . I have many reasons now to realize that I've lived out a fantasy in the longing that I would one day prepare for a night such as this. It must always have been in such situations that I imagined I could get lost in a person, that I'd brave a different kind of death entirely to remain with them. Perhaps that's why I'm being tugged into the room now by a force I can't resist. The appeal of living out a dream once more, in one's own fashion. I'm imbued with the joy of a journey I've longed for for years, unfulfilled.[21]

Still, on that long journey, I continued to carry inside me many abandoned texts, people, and possibilities, I steadily propagated sounds, faces, and relationships I thought could be shared; there were days when, in the name of a few bodies of text, I turned a blind eye to desperation, almost believing that I was living out certain possibilities. The prolonged lie was necessary, almost inevitable in order to latch onto life. As a matter of fact, distant cities, distant streets, and distant lives were always distant possibilities. Was everything a dream, in that case, one difficult to confess and accept? Had I experienced everything I depicted and depicted, clearly and wholeheartedly, all I had experienced? How much of my experiences in that faraway city years ago, or who knows, in the manuscript itself, has been left behind to me, how will I describe the residue those visions have left in me? Am I doing myself a great disservice by constantly dwelling on a dilemma and continually keeping it on my life's agenda? How many people are there at any point in this text who can share with me the evocations of a dilemma? Perhaps, in that case, I should refer to my ordeal as the enchantment of words. The enchantment of words, after all the years, indeed; the enchantment of words so we may, if silently, voyage in a dilemma without end. I feel as though I've used this phrase before in the name of another life or longing. At a time when all is indistinguishable from resentful, melancholy loving, if memory serves me well, I had claimed to be setting out on an indefinable pursuit. It was evening. It was time, once more, to return to a manuscript and a life. I was a prisoner to the trope of returning, I know. Perhaps, who knows, my insistence in trailing such a theme would be viewed as obsessive by others. Yet wasn't everyone prisoner to a handful of themes, scents, or emotions? That evening an old waiter had appealed to me in words that would take me years to make sense of, as though trying to give me the news, the story of a vague future. Yet ultimately, at least considering those days, affairs, and anxieties, for the telling of what story were my experiences a conduit? What incarnation of the old waiter had I brought to this ever-changing, self-transfiguring manuscript, from where and under what influence and future delusion had I carried these details?

Some small hope or the call of an unexpected vision

would then take me to a story that I somehow sensed would always be incomplete. After all those years the most I could speak of seemed to be fragmented memories and words. The story of an affair that gained meaning through its shortcomings, that was never completed, that I was in reality a little bit reluctant to complete . . . lives indistinguishable from resentments, remorse, and disappointment . . . regardless of all these words and lives, these emotions wouldn't let me be for years more still. I was reclining on a bed just like today. I can't express, even today, the feelings that the knock had provoked in me. Who had knocked on my door on that evening, who had called to me or wanted to? I could never answer this question, and I know I never will. Yet whatever the outcome, I had ostensibly set out on the journey of that story under the influence of such an absence of answers, constantly and hopefully striving to push the boundaries between reality and fiction. The story, the call without answers, had begun many years ago, and who knew for how long and in what fashion it would carry on?

That's why my reflection in the mirror frightens me once more. I'm not in a dream, to top it off; I'm obliged to assume everything, all resentments, offences, and possible disenchantments, whether I'd like to or not. To cross a threshold, to muster the strength, I say then to myself. To be able to continue, yes, continue for the sake of the allure of a story that won't and can't be told. In other words, I can't stop myself from progressing toward a loneliness I think I know too well, despite all its dangers: what was the wrong, the original wrong, that is to say, the wrong that brought us to this point, my love? In my search for you, for the sake of a hope I still decline to clarify? In my perpetuating an endless longing inside from a proclivity for always living this kind of love? In my habit of being able to engage my mechanism of self-deception even in the bleakest of situations? Or, all else aside, wasn't something ultimately wrong with all of this, or was all the chagrin to be viewed as the natural outcome of every possible, expected, and anticipated relationship? Questions, questions, questions. That must be the most important indication that we're headed toward a person, a person no matter who, if in unfavorable words. I may have numerous reasons to leave a manuscript unfinished, to refuse to finish it despite all the years. Who, after all, was ever able to write the final sentence, who could answer the questions, the real questions? The resentment of never being able to answer the questions adequately enough, indeed. Wasn't it a beginning, though, to show the courage to take on the questions no matter the risks, was it not a new departure after all those lives and forced returns to oneself?)

You also had words, evocations or merely questions in your life

Questions that you couldn't easily answer, and that you often avoided answering

Yet did these questions not lead you to other questions, to unexpected exits?

Were these not the very questions, in fact, that tethered us to life, sent us in pursuit of certain delayed answers?

Through these questions, did we not head toward new stories or people?

Were we not born with stories afresh, into possibilities afresh?

40
Eternal Game, Eternal Death

1. *ON ONE OF THOSE evenings that the little joys integral to passion seem to wear out more every day in spite of all delusions, you imagine, for instance, sipping on a local drink in a coffeehouse of an unfamiliar city. You know that the dream and the world you've constructed in your head are actually completely different from reality. You may hear, then, the vague notes of a song. You try to identify it, place it somewhere in your past. This too, however, is an illusion, to tell the truth, the effort to break free of hopelessness. As such, what do journeys matter really, what journey means an escape and from whom, from what disappointment or dilemma?*

2. *When one proliferated images, colors, sounds, and smells, did that then mean an unnecessary bludgeoning of one's brand-new options? Weren't you but the same extension of a shadow, increasingly its counterpart, in your aloneness in the city, watching the extraordinary sunset while you kept alive the bittersweet joy within against all odds? When you considered, while in that city, that your dream lover would never know of your existence, had you not had to accept once more your very memorable voyeurism?*

3. *Ultimately the possibility had always existed and would always remain. Besides, was this departure not part of the reason, in a familiar manner of speaking, for your existence, your pursuit for the identity that you must bear whether you want to or not? Was this not a dream nurtured with years-long writing projects, unfinished novels, and poems that came to mind unbidden?*

4. *It may have been only after you perceived such a lie, and wished to express your perceptiveness, that many stories concerned with evocations or the search for the enchantment of words sprang to your mind. For you to realize that words are much more dangerous than initially thought, on the other hand, you, like many others before you, had to endeavor, sooner or later, the attempt [essay]. In a way this meant the existence of a story within another story. As such, was it more important to be inside an attempt or to be living it out constantly, or to make do with ambiguous answers, to reach a wider band of friends and comrades in the name of that tremendously valued communion?*

5. *After all, the evocations of the word* proliferate *settled more acutely into your life with each passing day. You owed that to the poems that you read with always the same melancholy and let permeate your days one way or another, and the quotidian details that gained meaning through these poems. To proliferate, yes, proliferate in the face of all words, solitudes, and small deaths. To proliferate in spite of your lust that's capable of turning into hell, of those you left behind whether you wished to or not, and of those you simply can't seem to pursue. Had you not once dreamed of standing before a mirror and searching for a beyond?*

6. *Such situations may well warrant a dream, one that will keep coming back to you constantly, certainly. A dream, so that a long, long and often dangerous voyage may begin toward the limitlessness of poetry. A dream, with it the places, images and the endless and interminable questions that contribute to the construction of a manuscript that's gradually a narrative. Where, when, and for the sake of what hopes had those words begun, for instance, or had been endeavored? What truths had become tantamount to what regrets? What treachery or shortcoming did those phrases express?*

7. *The story had never been lived out extensively and never would be. To top it off, no one would be able to tell another's*

story the way it required. In that case, why the repetitive retellings, no matter what their label or nature, why the effort to share things?

8. *In what city, bed-and-breakfast room, or era were you living in that story? What fear, lost past or possibility did the woman express with her mysterious loquaciousness and appearance that would haunt you for years? What words pertaining to the woman had you forgotten or ignored, if involuntarily, or even altered? Had you gone out in that city and wandered the strange streets at night? Would the streets of your imagination gain completely different meaning through an enchantment, some small hope or an unexpected detail? Did you leave something behind in your very brief existence in the small room? Did the old woman really say that everyone lives in their own isolation, or did you put the words in her mouth, due somewhat to the indescribable pull of the story you were meaning to write?*

9. *Other stories, other longings, other lives entirely. But no matter what you did or wished to do, hadn't you always and unequivocally wanted to write the same story?*

10. *Would you really be able to relate, to share with your protagonists the fatigue, would you be able to bear other narratives into that story, in the name of obstinately maintaining a never-ending fantasy?*

11. *That right there could've been the call of a terrifying danger that one hoped always to ignore. Doubtless you were no stranger to such moments. Yet for how long would this solitude, by degrees this desperation, increase, in what people or words would it find itself repeated? For how long, in such a room of a bed-and-breakfast, would you keep running into this dead end or ghost?*

12. *Because some are able to live in projected words, the history of words becomes identical to the history of people, and it starts seeming as if you're forever postponing certain possibilities. The day comes when in another narrative you ask yourself*

how you know those people and where you experienced them. You are thus in an instant of no return and wish you could run as far away as you can from these words, from this ominous history. You know, in fact, you know very well the story of this escape. The story of an escape, a return to oneself: is it not merely another form of heading toward new delusions or, simply, illusions?

13. *You may at times like these, in your solitude, be forced to bear the pangs of intermittent appearances of a lost lover. The night pushes on in all its magic and hushed tempestuousness. Many images degrade into hallucinations, and gradually into a nightmare, on such nights. Has the lover stopped by this place, has she shared with another what you weren't able to share with her in this room?*

14. *You may stop by one of these rooms years later and find that the evocations of this return awaken in you stories you're utterly unprepared for and, even if for the duration of a writing adventure, the will to live again. You cannot stop diversifying these stories, proliferating them in your own way. So much that after a while it's neither here nor there that others interpret your attitude as obsessive. After all, for you, the faces drifting away in the flow of time and their residue in certain objects are worth keeping in the most private of memories and quietly bearing into another room or relationship. What relic, photograph, book or doodle can lead you to another, for example, or depict you to another in a singular language? In what resentments do you stop and spell out this prolonged adventure, after all the losses?*

15. *Evocations, evocations, evocations. Was the following phrase enough to touch upon that complicated world, even if fleetingly? Would the intoxication of a certain wine, a song or merely a smell not suffice to open the door to another memory? Besides, did everyone not experience different evocations with every image? Did the same word not act as a conduit to different clues in different worlds?*

16.   *Were you hounded by the anxiety of repeating yourself?
      Couldn't you instead just focus on autumn, a long, very long
      autumn?*

17.   *This story really would project itself into your consciousness
      for years to come. Cavafy, for instance, would multiply its
      various meanings within you and you would maintain those
      poems in the ways that you lived them, clandestinely, without
      pretense, only for yourself. You too had "invisible cities," and
      in them you could attempt, in your own way, "the story of a
      day." For in spite of all the poems you read and all the songs
      you heard about it, you seemed to be losing the city you were
      born and bred in more with each passing day. As such, that
      the loss was manifested through various people to confront
      you was the chief signifier of your desperation. Could you
      attempt to overcome it by pushing certain limits or by trying
      out certain discourses, at least for the duration of this act of
      writing, and more importantly, could you forget it?*

18.   *Perhaps right then you felt a breeze from that writer you love
      so much. No matter how much you wish to you could no
      longer distance certain influences, nor could you hide them
      from others. Was that the inevitable result of communica-
      tion, of the need to relate? Whereas once you yourself were a
      reader, faced with the obligation of entering a complicity, of
      sharing a life one way or another, through a body of text. The
      menace hadn't yet knocked on your door; you hadn't yet gone
      in search of that voice, those friends, those secret witnesses.
      That voice, yes, from that day on you'd clamor for that voice.
      That voice. Yet after so much searching, would you be able
      to define that voice to your heart's content?*

19.   *This was in fact an out-and-out dangerous adventure, one
      that would take heart. Yet ultimately everyone had their own
      voice to sound. Everyone had their own voice, their own call.
      Could the similarity between words, merely a handful of
      words, or a handful of images, and what you're experiencing
      today, not be salvation enough?*

20. *This was actually one of the unavoidable, predictable places that the little joys integral to passion can bring us against all delusions. You could call it experiencing or attempting to experience that lover years later once more, in an utterly dissimilar life. It must be an attempt tantamount to trailing an utterly, utterly dissimilar fantasy. Such a development, perhaps, was inevitable is this chapter of the story. You could now imagine yourself to have arrived on shore. What was the shore like that you left behind, however, could you return to that shore, would you wish you could? Was there another shore, if there was one left at all? After the shore, what kind of place would you go to? What kind of place would you go to?*

41
Old Games, Old Narratives

THAT MAY WELL BE the reason that we're forced now, years later, to review through different eyes this passion that came fully out of left field. At this point in the story, for instance, how are we to bear, or appear as though we bear, the resentment? By carrying on with the game as though nothing happened and no destruction or disillusionment took place? By withdrawing into a corner, in other words, by trying to come to terms once more with silence and as such delaying confrontation once more? By running the risk of putting salt in the wound or agreeing to tell the story sooner or later, to write the lover in with different places and different people entirely? I know this feeling of disillusionment, I remember it whether I would like to or not. In spite of all longing or hope it all looked wrong and inconsistent from the very beginning, yes. It was all wrong, because the Narrator had summoned a lover that had never existed in the way she was depicted in this text, in the way he longed for, with a sensitivity that would mean nothing to a prospective lover and a discourse that was nothing but its forced expression, a sum of unvaryingly suspicious words; he had, in spite of all his past experience, once more overlooked the fact that the loser in a relationship could never be effective, that no person was willing to give another affection, mere affection, just like that. To top it off, he hadn't even wanted to remember the importance of sexuality and sex appeal, or that vulgarity trumped sensitivity and aggression manifested in myriad ways was more impressive than a kind word. Our experiences in those old stories, on the other hand, had caused us to claim that we lived in a world that spun around the female genitalia.

All aside, with the scant data we have we can't even be sure if the lover really existed, or whether or not she heard the story. Even worse than that is that it's more or less impossible to make any further progress. After all, there are certain people who often afford to tell little lies in the name of certain experiences, in preparation for the relationships they long for. These little lies are really among the most indispensable refuges of the discordant and the perpetual prisoner of defeat. It changes nothing to claim you've also lived, once a discordant and you will always be a discordant, likewise once a contrarian always a contrarian, however, as I've mentioned, there are many reasons to cling to these bitter lies as though they were life buoys. When I consider the issue from such an angle, I can easily say that the Narrator has merely made up this passion in the name of living out his own story or delusion, that he has outright lied, in other words, that out of nowhere he got it into his head to become a writer. The attempt ought to be appraised as the unnecessary, meaningless venture it is. For one thing there's no sanctuary in authorship to take pride in, to covet or, above all, to impress a prospective lover. That aside, this deadly effort also contains the story of a secret that can't and won't be given to anyone, in spite of any synergy, an untold solitude, and the aloneness of that great, protracted journey. The issue of the way leading from apprenticeship to mastery, or to put it more accurately, from apprenticeship to apprenticeship. I don't think I need to say anything further.

Ultimately, as always and everywhere, there's another side to the coin. A bit of a stretch, admittedly, but this passion can also be seen as one that was endured in a story not easy to comprehend and thus not easy to stomach, for which the price, as explained, has been paid extensively. You may at this point have to blame everything on a moment of inattention and amnesia. The Narrator, whom I know, whom I have no doubt I know, must have been the victim of such passion only after so many years, season changes, songs, stories always told though unwritten, and journeys to the self. All things considered, however, it would do us good to remember that nothing in human relationships can ever be built on solid foundations, that in spite of any and all memories, there are traps against which one is unequipped to defend oneself. It's no small matter arguing against such a thought, especially when regarding passion. For we may once again be reminded of the theme of constantly wasting ourselves away in a journey or in another, as a fear we can't shake free of, an obsession in the eyes of some. That voice that constantly lives within us amongst silence and moves forward unceasingly now belongs to all of us. We're all, each in our own way, prisoner to our own imaginary passion or lover. It all begins again in the first words of a manuscript, on the dawn of a fresh new morning, an instant of pure joy, the first donning of an outfit, the scent of a flower, or a sea voyage. Until another new disappointment that one becomes inured to in time. Something thus always falls short in the construction of that little sanctuary. In that case we confront the fantasy with questions such as what kind of game was this, or who, under what conditions, was included in it? There's a shortfall, indeed, one that cannot be named. Yet if not for the hope we cultivated within due to that feeling of falling short, would you be able to fantasize to your heart's desire about a brand-new day dawning with its melancholy glimmer at the end of an injurious night?

42
That Spell, That Passion, That Deadly Journey

WHATEVER MAY BE WRITTEN or ruminated in these piecemeal texts, I must say loud and clear that I never intended to finish this story. I had many reasons, after all, to pick apart certain emotions, to leave relationships dragging, and to turn a blind eye to all of my self-evasions. That was why I turned constantly to certain phrases, continually pushed certain options and pursued certain words, obstinately, fearfully, and at times remorsefully. Afraid of all possible endings, I seek refuge in a dangerous fantasy. Words and the images they evoked may have been significant, who is to say, perhaps that was why they were important in my life. To never finish a long, extremely long-winded story, yes. It's a longing that was kept alive and chased after in nearly every manuscript, a variety of people and in the name of myriad dissimilar emotions, a longing that may only ultimately gain meaning through the narration of a delayed journey. For I believe, I want to believe with my very being, that this story, the origins of which remain elusive to me, may carry on in others as much as in me.

The adventure of faith, some small longing. This phrase feels to me like an appeal to scrutinize certain problems with the part up till this point or give living with my apprehensions another try, an irrevocability in which the game must somehow be sustained. In all honesty I can't say how necessary it is for me to point out at this point that all emotions are tantamount to preparation for a person, a lengthy narrative, or a journey. After all, I'm liable to be drawn any minute into futile, useless argument by many due to my

approach. What I wish to say is that everyone in their own
way is prisoner to a set of fears or apprehensions. To be perfectly honest, though, it altogether relieves me to think, to
each his own preparation and, even further, that this preparation is one of the most significant things that makes us
human, at least in the way I long for, and that life may gain
meaning through a state of constant preparation. All aside,
when I think back on all we've endured till today, the effort
to express things in accordance with a habitual system, dia-
chronically, seems to me an effort at self-delusion, as unwit-
ting as it may be. Putting aside my forced interventions with
fateful commentaries, leaving the narration as it is against
the risk of being accused of irresponsibility seems to me the
only way out.

The existence of such a way, however, still doesn't help
me solve every problem I have in my head. A friend I love
and, as strange as it may seem, also respect, had at a point
of preparation for this story that was very different from the
current one told me that an attempt at a story with the main
title "Prologue" could hinder the sense of incompleteness
by which I set so much store and, even further, at odds with
what was promised initially, could make what was expressed
seem somehow complete. In fact, the manuscript had been
designed at first as an independent story in itself but, due
to reasons that feel too superfluous to explain now, I was
unable to go along with certain deliberations that are now
long in the past. Believe me when I say that, approaching
the matter from the angle of these hesitations, I still can't
understand how I decided to include this text in the book
in its current incarnation. Indeed, what has been depicted
here may well be considered for a different book or placed in
this book in a different timeline entirely. Such an alteration
could bring with it disparate comments and emphases. For
now, however, I happen to have lost the opportunity. The rest
depends on those who are, in some way or another, fond of

games. More important than anything at this point, I suppose, is that I can fathom now that this manuscript has fulfilled an adventure through the flow of years, albeit mutedly,
that in spite of having been written a long, long time ago,
comes scarily close to my recent experiences, that it contains
clues regarding certain points that were left in the dark and,
most significantly, that it's on the cusp of branching out into
myriad possible future stories. It was from this realization
that the footnotes that some may find bizarre, superfluous
or outlandish stemmed. As such, quite to the contrary of
my friend's apprehensions, one gets the sense that the game
somehow continues and, who knows, may well never end.
There's no reason why these footnotes shouldn't branch out
into other footnotes eventually. It's an old, age-old game,
naturally, one in which I cannot stop playing protagonist
or walking alongside certain old-time comrades.

Games, yes, games with no end in sight. I suppose at this
stage I can dwell on your second question that has kept me
preoccupied for some time. A friend of mine, whose opinion
I'm fond of because he has no fear of long sentences, has no
qualms about laconically expressing his mood even in the
most inappropriate setting by yelling, "I feel like donkey,
I feel like donkey," mastered conversational Italian in the
fifteen days he spent in Florence, wants to be cremated, goes
to the synagogue only for the funerals of beloved friends
despite his devout upbringing, and boasts having given his
goatee a Bar Mitzvah, on an evening he was making his
opinions on this story known with his exceptional talent for
digression told me, as though imparting a hugely important secret, that I ought to flesh it out with some historical
context, because otherwise it may resemble the love stories
of Necati Özgül Karaboduroğlu. I was obligated in those
days to peruse all of my options and push every possible
limit. The manuscript itself would eventually reveal the
rights and wrongs, after all. That was why I tried to dwell

on the historical context suggested by my friend in spite of
all my doubts. I say doubts, because in literary works which
take history as a determinant and, even more importantly,
as an ideal, I've always preferred to hunt for entirely different, singular details. For some reason I've always found it
laughable for a writer to work with the meticulousness of
a historian, or at least claim to do so. Still, for the melan-
cholic backtracking in the "Epilogue" chapter, I could have
in that context found an interesting backdrop. For instance,
I could've easily picked a writer who, unable to withstand
the political pressure in his country, makes the conscious
decision to emigrate to another land, irrevocably crestfallen
and forever leaving behind in each country he visits part of
his hope. The events of the recent few years in the land we
inhabit could very well present a basis for such a design. For
the realization of this, however, truth be told, one needed
neither to be the narrator of an era nor to write a book as
thick as a brick. As for discussions regarding the author's
function, duty or leadership, one must sadly only smile in
return, resentfully, hopelessly, forever bearing the brunt of
that terrible sense of isolation. No matter what they may
seek to establish or, in more crude terms, to foist off on the
unsuspecting, this is an opportunity, of course, to repeat
that the adventure of writing is a very quiet one, that the
games endeavored in this adventure can be played with a
very select few. As such the only things left are the pursuit of various details and narrating the process of giving it
meaning. All of this adds up to the predicament, naturally,
that the prisoners of such manuscripts must be ready at all
times for an isolation without end. There's no point at all,
in other words, in waiting for that lover, longing for that
passion, or departing for that country. That's the very context for all that I wanted to write initially, but chose not to,
gaining meaning. It may well be another way of avoiding to
the best of my means the trap of conformity. Perhaps none

of what happened here had any secret meaning, message or objective. What was depicted here neither alluded to the life of some obscure acquaintance of yours nor any autobiographical details. None of what was depicted here aimed at a certain ending, or a certain genre or a covert call to a person. Certain people roughly described here and there in the manuscript had been picked somewhat deliberately, to cause confusion. Depicting Istanbul was, in this manuscript as in others, an irrevocability, no, an obligation, but in a similar attempt that may be undertaken in a few years, there were myriad reasons to pick another city. As for turns of phrase, I suppose the best course of action at this point, in spite of any assumptions or longings, is to remember that everyone has only one phrase and to believe that the communion of these phrases will sooner or later result in a never-ending, never-fading body of text. After all, to voyage out one must have faith in the existence of such possibilities. At some point in this prolonged path, however, are also bound to be journeys of silence that one chooses in the face of this old dream and cannot share with another. At that you are compelled to relive that pause, that long solitude, and are suffused with familiar melancholy. That's why I can't say whether in time I'll want to return to these writings, or show the courage to join your ranks once more. Yet it's in your hands to carry on, to contribute to this story that doesn't look as though it will end anytime soon. I know it's a difficult endeavor. For there's nothing quite like the resistance of words and the secret rebellion between parentheses. A challenging, often deadly struggle for survival, yes. When we choose to forever be on the road, or to put it more accurately, when we long to, we have no other choice, nor should we have; there is no other tunnel, possible exit door or meetings in the sanctuary, and considering our imprisonment in solitude, nor should there be. Yet is this an evasion, a new struggle to hide oneself, or an attempt to search for oneself? Never mind. Carry on your path as though nothing has happened and nothing will. If you ask me, this is your time to go under that spell. That spell, that passion, that deadly journey. Listen, listen well, this story is yours. Do you hear the sirens?

Born in 1957, MARIO LEVI graduated from the University of Istanbul Faculty of Literature in 1980 with a degree in French language and literature. He has published two story collections and four novels. In addition to being a writer, he has worked as a French teacher, an importer, a journalist, a radio programmer, and a copywriter. He currently lectures at Yeditepe University.

ZEYNEP BELER is a translator of Turkish-language literature. Among the authors she has translated are Ece Temelkuran and Hakan Günday. She lives in Istanbul.

MICHAL AJVAZ, *The Golden Age.*
The Other City.
PIERRE ALBERT-BIROT, *Grabinoulor.*
YUZ ALESHKOVSKY, *Kangaroo.*
SVETLANA ALEXIEVICH, *Voices from Chernobyl.*
FELIPE ALFAU, *Chromos.*
Locos.
JOAO ALMINO, *Enigmas of Spring.*
IVAN ÂNGELO, *The Celebration.*
The Tower of Glass.
ANTÓNIO LOBO ANTUNES, *Knowledge of Hell.*
The Splendor of Portugal.
ALAIN ARIAS-MISSON, *Theatre of Incest.*
JOHN ASHBERY & JAMES SCHUYLER, *A Nest of Ninnies.*
GABRIELA AVIGUR-ROTEM, *Heatwave and Crazy Birds.*
DJUNA BARNES, *Ladies Almanack.*
Ryder.
JOHN BARTH, *Letters.*
Sabbatical.
Collected Stories.
DONALD BARTHELME, *The King.*
Paradise.
SVETISLAV BASARA, *Chinese Letter.*
Fata Morgana.
In Search of the Grail.
MIQUEL BAUÇÀ, *The Siege in the Room.*
RENÉ BELLETTO, *Dying.*
MAREK BIENCZYK, *Transparency.*
ANDREI BITOV, *Pushkin House.*
ANDREJ BLATNIK, *You Do Understand.*
Law of Desire.
LOUIS PAUL BOON, *Chapel Road.*
My Little War.
Summer in Termuren.
ROGER BOYLAN, *Killoyle.*
IGNÁCIO DE LOYOLA BRANDÃO, *Anonymous Celebrity.*
Zero.
BRIGID BROPHY, *In Transit.*
The Prancing Novelist.

GABRIELLE BURTON, *Heartbreak Hotel.*
MICHEL BUTOR, *Degrees.*
Mobile.
G. CABRERA INFANTE, *Infante's Inferno.*
Three Trapped Tigers.
JULIETA CAMPOS, *The Fear of Losing Eurydice.*
ANNE CARSON, *Eros the Bittersweet.*
ORLY CASTEL-BLOOM, *Dolly City.*
LOUIS-FERDINAND CÉLINE, *North.*
Conversations with Professor Y.
London Bridge.
HUGO CHARTERIS, *The Tide Is Right.*
ERIC CHEVILLARD, *Demolishing Nisard.*
The Author and Me.
MARC CHOLODENKO, *Mordechai Schamz.*
EMILY HOLMES COLEMAN, *The Shutter of Snow.*
ERIC CHEVILLARD, *The Author and Me.*
LUIS CHITARRONI, *The No Variations.*
CH'OE YUN, *Mannequin.*
ROBERT COOVER, *A Night at the Movies.*
STANLEY CRAWFORD, *Log of the S.S. The Mrs Unguentine.*
Some Instructions to My Wife.
RALPH CUSACK, *Cadenza.*
NICHOLAS DELBANCO, *Sherbrookes.*
The Count of Concord.
NIGEL DENNIS, *Cards of Identity.*
PETER DIMOCK, *A Short Rhetoric for Leaving the Family.*
ARIEL DORFMAN, *Konfidenz.*
COLEMAN DOWELL, *Island People.*
Too Much Flesh and Jabez.
RIKKI DUCORNET, *Phosphor in Dreamland.*
The Complete Butcher's Tales.
RIKKI DUCORNET (cont.), *The Jade Cabinet.*
The Fountains of Neptune.
WILLIAM EASTLAKE, *Castle Keep.*
Lyric of the Circle Heart.
JEAN ECHENOZ, *Chopin's Move.*

STANLEY ELKIN, *A Bad Man.*
The Dick Gibson Show.
The Franchiser.

FRANÇOIS EMMANUEL, *Invitation to a Voyage.*

SALVADOR ESPRIU, *Ariadne in the Grotesque Labyrinth.*

LESLIE A. FIEDLER, *Love and Death in the American Novel.*

JUAN FILLOY, *Op Oloop.*

GUSTAVE FLAUBERT, *Bouvard and Pécuchet.*

JON FOSSE, *Aliss at the Fire.*
Melancholy.
Trilogy.

FORD MADOX FORD, *The March of Literature.*

MAX FRISCH, *I'm Not Stiller.*
Man in the Holocene.

CARLOS FUENTES, *Christopher Unborn.*
Distant Relations.
Terra Nostra.
Where the Air Is Clear.
Nietzsche on His Balcony.

WILLIAM GADDIS, JR., *The Recognitions.*
JR.

JANICE GALLOWAY, *Foreign Parts.*
The Trick Is to Keep Breathing.

WILLIAM H. GASS, *Life Sentences.*
The Tunnel.
The World Within the Word.
Willie Masters' Lonesome Wife.

GÉRARD GAVARRY, *Hoppla! 1 2 3.*

ETIENNE GILSON, *The Arts of the Beautiful.*
Forms and Substances in the Arts.

C. S. GISCOMBE, *Giscome Road.*
Here.

DOUGLAS GLOVER, *Bad News of the Heart.*

WITOLD GOMBROWICZ, *A Kind of Testament.*

PAULO EMÍLIO SALES GOMES, *P's Three Women.*

GEORGI GOSPODINOV, *Natural Novel.*

JUAN GOYTISOLO, *Juan the Landless.*
Makbara.
Marks of Identity.

JACK GREEN, *Fire the Bastards!*

JIŘÍ GRUŠA, *The Questionnaire.*

MELA HARTWIG, *Am I a Redundant Human Being?*

JOHN HAWKES, *The Passion Artist.*
Whistlejacket.

ELIZABETH HEIGHWAY, ED., *Contemporary Georgian Fiction.*

AIDAN HIGGINS, *Balcony of Europe.*
Blind Man's Bluff.
Bornholm Night-Ferry.
Langrishe, Go Down.
Scenes from a Receding Past.

ALDOUS HUXLEY, *Antic Hay.*
Point Counter Point.
Those Barren Leaves.
Time Must Have a Stop.

JANG JUNG-IL, *When Adam Opens His Eyes*

DRAGO JANČAR, *The Tree with No Name.*
I Saw Her That Night.
Galley Slave.

MIKHEIL JAVAKHISHVILI, *Kvachi.*

GERT JONKE, *The Distant Sound.*
Homage to Czerny.
The System of Vienna.

JACQUES JOUET, *Mountain R.*
Savage.
Upstaged.

JUNG YOUNG-MOON, *A Contrived World.*

MIEKO KANAI, *The Word Book.*

YORAM KANIUK, *Life on Sandpaper.*

ZURAB KARUMIDZE, *Dagny.*

PABLO KATCHADJIAN, *What to Do.*

JOHN KELLY, *From Out of the City.*

HUGH KENNER, *Flaubert, Joyce and Beckett: The Stoic Comedians.*
Joyce's Voices.

DANILO KIŠ, *The Attic.*
The Lute and the Scars.
Psalm 44.
A Tomb for Boris Davidovich.

ANITA KONKKA, *A Fool's Paradise.*

GEORGE KONRÁD, *The City Builder.*

TADEUSZ KONWICKI, *A Minor Apocalypse.*

The Polish Complex.

ELAINE KRAF, *The Princess of 72nd Street.*

JIM KRUSOE, *Iceland.*

AYSE KULIN, *Farewell: A Mansion in Occupied Istanbul.*

EMILIO LASCANO TEGUI, *On Elegance While Sleeping.*

ERIC LAURRENT, *Do Not Touch.*

VIOLETTE LEDUC, *La Bâtarde.*

LEE KI-HO, *At Least We Can Apologize.*

EDOUARD LEVÉ, *Autoportrait.*

Suicide.

MARIO LEVI, *Istanbul Was a Fairy Tale.*

DEBORAH LEVY, *Billy and Girl.*

JOSÉ LEZAMA LIMA, *Paradiso.*

OSMAN LINS, *Avalovara.*

The Queen of the Prisons of Greece.

ALF MACLOCHLAINN, *Out of Focus.*

Past Habitual.

RON LOEWINSOHN, *Magnetic Field(s).*

YURI LOTMAN, *Non-Memoirs.*

D. KEITH MANO, *Take Five.*

MINA LOY, *Stories and Essays of Mina Loy.*

MICHELINE AHARONIAN MARCOM, *The Mirror in the Well.*

BEN MARCUS, *The Age of Wire and String.*

WALLACE MARKFIELD, *Teitlebaum's Window.*

To an Early Grave.

DAVID MARKSON, *Reader's Block.*

Wittgenstein's Mistress.

CAROLE MASO, *AVA.*

HISAKI MATSUURA, *Triangle.*

LADISLAV MATEJKA & KRYSTYNA POMORSKA, EDS., *Readings in Russian Poetics: Formalist & Structuralist Views.*

HARRY MATHEWS, *Cigarettes.*

The Conversions.

The Human Country.

The Journalist.

My Life in CIA.

Singular Pleasures.

The Sinking of the Odradek.

Stadium.

Tlooth.

JOSEPH MCELROY, *Night Soul and Other Stories.*

ABDELWAHAB MEDDEB, *Talismano.*

GERHARD MEIER, *Isle of the Dead.*

HERMAN MELVILLE, *The Confidence-Man.*

AMANDA MICHALOPOULOU, *I'd Like.*

STEVEN MILLHAUSER, *The Barnum Museum.*

In the Penny Arcade.

RALPH J. MILLS, JR., *Essays on Poetry.*

CHRISTINE MONTALBETTI, *The Origin of Man.*

Western.

NICHOLAS MOSLEY, *Accident.*

Assassins.

Catastrophe Practice.

Hopeful Monsters.

Imago Bird.

Natalie Natalia.

Serpent.

WARREN MOTTE, *Fiction Now: The French Novel in the 21st Century.*

Oulipo: A Primer of Potential Literature.

GERALD MURNANE, *Barley Patch.*

Inland.

YVES NAVARRE, *Our Share of Time.*

Sweet Tooth.

DOROTHY NELSON, *In Night's City.*

Tar and Feathers.

WILFRIDO D. NOLLEDO, *But for the Lovers.*

BORIS A. NOVAK, *The Master of Insomnia.*

FLANN O'BRIEN, *At Swim-Two-Birds.*

The Best of Myles.

The Dalkey Archive.

The Hard Life.

The Poor Mouth.

The Third Policeman.

CLAUDE OLLIER, *The Mise-en-Scène.*

Wert and the Life Without End.

PATRIK OUŘEDNÍK, *Europeana.*
The Opportune Moment, 1855.

BORIS PAHOR, *Necropolis.*

FERNANDO DEL PASO, *News from the Empire.*
Palinuro of Mexico.

ROBERT PINGET, *The Inquisitory.*
Mahu or The Material.
Trio.

MANUEL PUIG, *Betrayed by Rita Hayworth.*
The Buenos Aires Affair.
Heartbreak Tango.

RAYMOND QUENEAU, *The Last Days.*
Odile.
Pierrot Mon Ami.
Saint Glinglin.

ANN QUIN, *Berg.*
Passages.
Three.
Tripticks.

ISHMAEL REED, *The Free-Lance Pallbearers.*
The Last Days of Louisiana Red.
Ishmael Reed: The Plays.
Juice!
The Terrible Threes.
The Terrible Twos.
Yellow Back Radio Broke-Down.

RAINER MARIA RILKE,
The Notebooks of Malte Laurids Brigge.

JULIÁN RÍOS, *The House of Ulysses.*
Larva: A Midsummer Night's Babel.
Poundemonium.

ALAIN ROBBE-GRILLET, *Project for a Revolution in New York.*
A Sentimental Novel.

AUGUSTO ROA BASTOS, *I the Supreme.*

DANIËL ROBBERECHTS, *Arriving in Avignon.*

JEAN ROLIN, *The Explosion of the Radiator Hose.*

OLIVIER ROLIN, *Hotel Crystal.*

ALIX CLEO ROUBAUD, *Alix's Journal.*

JACQUES ROUBAUD, *The Form of a City Changes Faster, Alas, Than the Human Heart.*

The Great Fire of London.
Hortense in Exile.
Hortense Is Abducted.
Mathematics: The Plurality of Worlds of Lewis.
Some Thing Black.

RAYMOND ROUSSEL, *Impressions of Africa.*

VEDRANA RUDAN, *Night.*

GERMAN SADULAEV, *The Maya Pill.*

TOMAŽ ŠALAMUN, *Soy Realidad.*

LYDIE SALVAYRE, *The Company of Ghosts.*

LUIS RAFAEL SÁNCHEZ, *Macho Camacho's Beat.*

SEVERO SARDUY, *Cobra & Maitreya.*

NATHALIE SARRAUTE, *Do You Hear Them?*
Martereau.
The Planetarium.

STIG SÆTERBAKKEN, *Siamese.*
Self-Control.
Through the Night.

ARNO SCHMIDT, *Collected Novellas.*
Collected Stories.
Nobodaddy's Children.
Two Novels.

ASAF SCHURR, *Motti.*

GAIL SCOTT, *My Paris.*

JUNE AKERS SEESE,
Is This What Other Women Feel Too?

BERNARD SHARE, *Inish.*
Transit.

VIKTOR SHKLOVSKY, *Bowstring.*
Literature and Cinematography.
Theory of Prose.
Third Factory.
Zoo, or Letters Not about Love.

PIERRE SINIAC, *The Collaborators.*

KJERSTI A. SKOMSVOLD,
The Faster I Walk, the Smaller I Am.

JOSEF ŠKVORECKÝ, *The Engineer of Human Souls.*

GILBERT SORRENTINO, *Aberration of Starlight.*
Blue Pastoral.
Crystal Vision.

Imaginative Qualities of Actual Things.
Mulligan Stew.
Red the Fiend.
Steelwork.
Under the Shadow.
ANDRZEJ STASIUK, *Dukla.*
Fado.
GERTRUDE STEIN, *The Making of Americans.*
A Novel of Thank You.
PIOTR SZEWC, *Annihilation.*
GONÇALO M. TAVARES, *A Man: Klaus Klump.*
Jerusalem.
Learning to Pray in the Age of Technique.
LUCIAN DAN TEODOROVICI, *Our Circus Presents...*
NIKANOR TERATOLOGEN, *Assisted Living.*
STEFAN THEMERSON, *Hobson's Island.*
The Mystery of the Sardine.
Tom Harris.
JOHN TOOMEY, *Sleepwalker.*
Huddleston Road.
Slipping.
DUMITRU TSEPENEAG, *Hotel Europa.*
The Necessary Marriage.
Pigeon Post.
Vain Art of the Fugue.
La Belle Roumaine.
Waiting: Stories.
ESTHER TUSQUETS, *Stranded.*
DUBRAVKA UGRESIC, *Lend Me Your Character.*
Thank You for Not Reading.
TOR ULVEN, *Replacement.*
MATI UNT, *Brecht at Night.*
Diary of a Blood Donor.
Things in the Night.
ÁLVARO URIBE & OLIVIA SEARS, EDS., *Best of Contemporary Mexican Fiction.*
ELOY URROZ, *Friction.*
The Obstacles.
LUISA VALENZUELA, *Dark Desires and the Others.*
He Who Searches.

PAUL VERHAEGHEN, *Omega Minor.*
BORIS VIAN, *Heartsnatcher.*
TOOMAS VINT, *An Unending Landscape.*
ORNELA VORPSI, *The Country Where No One Ever Dies.*
AUSTRYN WAINHOUSE, *Hedyphagetica.*
MARKUS WERNER, *Cold Shoulder.*
Zundel's Exit.
CURTIS WHITE, *The Idea of Home.*
Memories of My Father Watching TV.
Requiem.
DIANE WILLIAMS, *Excitability: Selected Stories.*
DOUGLAS WOOLF, *Wall to Wall.*
Ya! & John-Juan.
JAY WRIGHT, *Polynomials and Pollen.*
The Presentable Art of Reading Absence.
PHILIP WYLIE, *Generation of Vipers.*
MARGUERITE YOUNG, *Angel in the Forest.*
Miss MacIntosh, My Darling.
REYOUNG, *Unbabbling.*
ZORAN ŽIVKOVIĆ , *Hidden Camera.*
LOUIS ZUKOFSKY, *Collected Fiction.*
VITOMIL ZUPAN, *Minuet for Guitar.*
SCOTT ZWIREN, *God Head.*

AND MORE...